LEAPFROGS

Jim Hall

A & C Black • London

First published 1997 by
A & C Black Publishers Ltd
37 Soho Square, London W1D 3QZ
www.acblack.com

Reprinted 2005
Second edition 2002
First edition 1997
© 2002, 1997 Jim Hall

ISBN 0 7136 6398 7

A CIP catalogue record for this book
is available from the British Library.

Cover illustration by Eleanor King
Cover design by James Watson

A & C Black uses paper produced with elemental chlorine-free pulp,
harvested from managed sustainable forests.

Printed and bound in Great Britain by CPI Bath.

Contents

Introduction

Dance has a special place in primary school Physical Education because it is intensely physical, sociable, co-operative, creative and expressive. Dance is also great fun and a source of enjoyment for pupils.

The lively, physical nature of Dance is particularly valuable now, when children's life-styles have become increasingly sedentary and inactive. Well-organised lessons should be vigorous, active and non-stop, because the actions being performed are natural and easy. There are none of the problems encountered when controlling Games implements. There is no potential break in the flow of the lesson as when organising Gymnastic apparatus. In Dance, the teacher should be able to make his or her lessons 'scenes of busy activity.'

It has been said 'If you have never created something, you have never experienced a true sense of contentment.' Creativity is an ever-present feature of Dance and the wise teacher will always recognise, share and praise such achievement.

Teachers with little interest in Physical Education often admit to being impressed by the amount of language heard, used, understood and learned by pupils during Physical Education lessons. This discovery has been a stimulus to those teachers in their subsequent teaching of the subject.

Happily, the 1999 revised version of the Physical Education National Curriculum still requires schools to include both creative and traditional folk dance. The latter almost completely disappeared during the '60s and '70s when education lecturers called folk dance 'quite unsuitable' for primary school pupils because the steps and patterns 'belong to the adult world.'

Whether we are teaching creative or traditional dance, both teacher and class must have a definite 'goal' so that practising can become focused, repeatable, performable – and done expressively, with total commitment and involvement. The challenge to 'find ways to balance', for example, becomes much more exciting and 'real' when the outcome is the tightrope walker in the circus with all the dangerous, unsteady, wobbling about in space.

The book is designed to provide lots of ideas and practical help to the non-specialist class teacher. It recognises that each revised and reduced version of the NC provides less material, practical help and guidance regarding the content of dance and less help with the nature of good teaching practice in physical education. The 'Lesson Notes and NC Guidance' notes that accompany lessons aim to translate Programme of Study, Attainment Target and Learning across the National Curriculum elements into easily understandable objectives as well as giving practical help and guidance with the understanding, organising and teaching of the lessons.

The aims of Dance

1 *Dance is physical and we aim to make lessons physically challenging.* The focus is on the body and the development of well-controlled, poised, versatile movement. Vigorous actions also develop strength and flexibility and promote normal, healthy growth and development.

2 *Dance is creative and we aim to let pupils use their imagination.* Using imagination and skill to plan and present something original makes Dance a most satisfying activity. When a pupil's capacity for creative thinking and action is recognised and appreciated by the teacher, and shared with the class, this can increase self-confidence and self-esteem.

3 *Dance is expressive and communicative, and we aim to let pupils express their inner feelings through outward movement.* We use our bodies to 'express and communicate ideas' (NC Programme of Study). Feelings are expressed through body movement, as in angry stamping of feet; joyful gesturing of arms – 'Goal!'; fear, with its right withdrawal of the whole body; or the swaggering shoulders and strides of the over-confident.

4 *Dance is artistic and we aim to include variety and contrasts in every lesson.* Knowledge and understanding of the elements that enhance the quality of a performance need to be taught, and they contribute to a pupil's artistic education. Variety and contrast in the use of body action, shape, speed, force, level and direction are major contributors to improved quality.

5 *Dance is sociable, friendly and co-operative and we aim to let pupils work alone, with a partner and in groups in a variety of roles.* Because movement is natural, without the difficulty of controlling unpredictable Games implements or negotiating Gymnastic apparatus, success is quickly achieved. This achievement is often shared with a partner or group, leading to a strong sense of 'togetherness': unselfish sharing of space; taking turns; demonstrating to and being demonstrated to; and being appreciated and helped by others' comments are all typical of Dance teaching.

6 *Dance is fun and we aim to make enjoyment a constant feature.* Enjoyment from being praised for achievement; from participating and interacting in such an interesting and sociable activity; and from feeling and looking better after exercise, can all have a significant influence on peoples' eventual choice of lifestyles in years to come.

Developing Dance movement

To avoid confusion, the teacher will be thinking about, looking for, and talking about one element of movement at a time. In the early stages of a lesson's development, the teacher should only look at the actions and how the body parts concerned perform them. This allows an opportunity for progress and improvement. If, however, the teacher is exhorting the class to think about 'your spacing, actions, shape, speed – and what about some direction changes?', all at the same time, then confusion will be the only outcome.

Stage 1   The Body
What is the child doing?

1 *Actions* – travelling, jumping, turning, rolling, balancing, gesturing, rising, falling, etc.
2 *Body parts* – legs, feet, hands, shoulders, head, etc.
3 *Body shape* – stretched, curled, wide, twisted, arched.

Stage 2   The Space
Where is the child doing it?

1 *Directions* – forwards, backwards, sideways.
2 *Level* – high, medium, low.
3 *Size* – own, little, personal space; whole room, large, general space, shared with others.

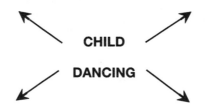

CHILD

DANCING

Stage 3   The Quality
How is the child doing it?

1 *Weight or effort* – firm, strong, vigorous, heavy.
2 *Time or speed* – sudden, fast, explosive, speeding up; slow, still, slowing down.

Stage 4   The Relationships
With whom is the child doing it?

1 *Alone* – but always conscious of sharing space with others.
2 *Teacher* – near, following, mirroring, in circle with, away from, back towards.
3 *Partner* – leading, following, meeting, parting, mirroring, copying, touching.
4 *Group* – circle, part of class for a demonstration.

Examples of Dance lesson development

If the class teacher feels confident about progressing the dance beyond the Stage 1 question 'What actions is the child doing?', the supplementary questions are those we should ask when observing movement.

Stage 1 *What are the body parts doing? What shapes are being used?*
Autumn Leaves The whole body makes the leaf shape which may have parts curling in, parts sticking out; be both smooth and crinkly.
Puppet Makers The puppet's arms can bend, swing, circle or reach up into a long or wide, stretched shape.
Fireworks The arms can reach forwards to give the whole body a streamlined, rocket shape.

Stage 2 *Where are we doing the dance? The floor is our stage – how are we using it to make our dance more interesting and exciting?*
Autumn Leaves As they fly they will sometimes soar from low to high; rotate in the same space; hover, hardly moving; glide to a far corner; drop straight, or with a spiralling action.
Puppet Makers Will show their puppets how hands and arms can reach into the space in front, at the side, behind and overhead.
Fireworks The rocket's straight swoosh contrasting with the spinning, circling of the Catherine wheel, and the unpredictable, variable jumping and shifting of the bangers.

Stage 3 *How are the movements being performed? Are the right amounts of force, effort, speed and quality factors being applied to make the performance particularly attractive, surprising, expressive?*
Autumn Leaves The gentle, slow, rise and fall, still attached to the branch contrasts with the sudden, almost explosive snap and break away from the branch.
Puppet Makers Arms can circle and swing, gently and softly, or they can punch and gesture in the air space, firmly and strongly.
Fireworks The long, smooth, ongoing, neat zoom of the rising rocket contrasts with sudden, explosive, fragmented scattering.

Stage 4 *With whom are we dancing? What are our relationships with the others in the room?*
Autumn Leaves An individual dance but we share the space with others as we weave, swoop, soar, hover, glide, tilt and turn, in and out, alongside or around them.
Puppet Makers Puppet and maker mirror each other on the spot, lead and follow, or are attached with strings in the travelling.
Fireworks One group at a time performs until spent, together, in the bonfire. All combine to flicker and sparkle in the fire, and interweave, flickering, shooting, crackling, subsiding, dying.

'The Government believes that two hours of physical activity a week, including the National Curriculum for physical education and extra-curricular activities, should be an aspiration for all schools. This applies to all key stages.'

Programme of Study

Pupils should be taught to:

a use movements imaginatively, responding to stimuli, including music, and performing basic skills (e.g. travelling, being still, making a shape, jumping, turning, gesturing).

b change the rhythm, speed, level and direction of their movements.

c create and perform dances using simple movement patterns, including those from different times and cultures.

d express and communicate ideas and feelings.

Attainment Target

Pupils should be able to demonstrate that they can:

a select and use skills, actions and ideas appropriately, applying them with co-ordination and control.

b copy, explore, repeat and remember skills, and link them in ways that suit the activities.

c talk about differences between their and others' work; suggest improvements; and use this understanding to improve their performance.

Main NC Headings when considering progression and expectation

* *Planning* – mostly before performing, but planning also takes place during performance, making quick decisions to find space or adapt a skill. In these initial, exploratory stages, pupils try things out and learn from early efforts. When planning is satisfactory, there is evidence of understanding of the task; good use of own ideas; and consideration for others sharing the space.

* *Performing and improving performance* – always the main outcome to be pursued and achieved. When performing is satisfactory, there is evidence of well-controlled, neat, safe and thoughtful work; a capacity for almost non-stop work, alone and with others; and simple skills being performed accurately and linked together with increasing control.

* *Linking actions* – pupils build longer, 'joined-up' sequences of linked actions in response to the task set and the stimuli used. In the same way that joined-up words make language and joined-up notes make music, joined-up actions produce movement sequences, ideally with a clear and obvious beginning, middle and end, like a sentence.

* *Reflecting and making judgements* – pupils describe what they and others have done; talk about what they liked in a performance; and then make practical use of this reflection to improve. Where standards in evaluating are satisfactory, there is evidence of accurate observation and awareness of the actions; understanding of differences and similarities seen in demonstrations; awareness of key features and ways to achieve and improve them; and sensitive concern for others' feelings when discussing their work.

Example of a checklist

CLASS: Y1 LESSON: September THEME: Body parts awareness	WARM-UP	MOVEMENT SKILLS TRAINING	CREATED DANCE
Plan and perform simple skills safely, showing control in linking actions together	✔	✔	✔
Improve performance by practising skills, alone and with a partner	✔	✔	✔
Learn to travel, jump, turn, gesture and be still, with control, balance and poise	✔	✔	✔
Perform patterns or movements including some traditional dances	✔	✔	✔
Express and communicate ideas and feelings	✔	✔	✔
Develop rhythmic responses with contrasts of speed, shape, level and direction	✔	✔	✔
Talk about own and others' performance and make simple judgements	✔	✔	✔

Teaching methods

Enthusiastic teaching is the main inspiration behind a successful lesson and usually creates an equally enthusiastic response in pupils.

The lesson plan is the busy teacher's essential guide. Failure to work from a written-down plan can result in repetition of lessons. July's lesson will only be more advanced than the previous September's if all the lessons in between have been recorded and referred to.

Shared choice or indirect teaching is the lesson plan most often used. The teacher decides the nature of the activity and challenges the class to decide on the actions.... 'As you travel and stop to my tambourine beat, can you show me varied travelling actions, and clear, still body shapes?'

Shared choice teaching with its 'Can you show me....?' approach produces a wide variety of results to add to the repertoire of both class and teacher. The NC requirement that pupils should be able to demonstrate that they can plan and 'use skills, actions and ideas appropriately' is best achieved through shared choice.

Direct teaching takes place when the teacher tells the class what to do. For example .... 'Skip to visit every part of the room'.... 'Stand with feet apart. Slowly stretch your arms high above your head.' If the class are restless, unresponsive or doing poor work, a directed activity can restore interest and discipline, and provide ideas and starting points from which to develop. Less creative pupils will benefit from direct teaching.

Pupil demonstrations are essential teaching aids because we remember what we see – good quality, safe, correct ways to perform; the exact meanings of Dance terminology; and good examples of variety and interesting contrasts. Occasional pupil demonstrations with follow-up comments by the observing pupils often bring out points not noticed by the teacher. Making friendly, encouraging, helpful comments to classmates is good for class morale and for extending the class repertoire.

'Be found working, not waiting' is a motto the class should have been trained to understand and pursue in order to enjoy satisfactory lessons with sufficient time for the creative dance which is the climax of the lesson.

Praise and recognition of progress and good work are important teaching aids, particularly when given with enthusiasm. Words of praise should be specific beacuse they are heard by all and remind the class of the main points.... 'Well done, Emma. Your floating snowflake movement was light and gentle.'

Assessment

There are three main requirements within the Attainment Target to concentrate on when assessing achievement. The dual emphasis on both performing and learning involves pupils in the continuous, inter-related process of:

Planning   Performing   Reflecting/Evaluating

Planning provides the focus and the concentrated thinking necessary for an accurate performance. It takes place both before and during performances, and subsequent performances are influenced by the planning that takes place after individuals and the group reflect on the success or otherwise of the activity.

Where planning standards are satisfactory, there is evidence of:

a thinking ahead and visualising the intended outcome

b originality and variety – individual ideas

c unselfish, considerate sharing of space

d positive personal qualities such as enthusiasm, concentration, and wholehearted involvement

e a clear understanding of the task

f good judgements being made.

Performing is the most important feature. We are fortunate that the visual nature of Physical Education enables pupils' achievements to be easily seen and judged.

When standards in performing are satisfactory, there is evidence of:

a neat, accurate, 'correct' performances

b successful, safe outcomes

c originality and versatility

d consistency and the ability to repeat and remember

e adaptability, making sudden adjustments as required

f economy of effort, making everything look 'easy.'

Reflecting and evaluating are important because they help both the performers and the observers with their further planning, preparation, adaptation and improvement.

When standards in evaluating are satisfactory, pupils are able to:

a observe accurately and pick out key features

b make encouraging, helpful comments about a performance

c make comparisons between two or more performers

d comment on the 'correctness' of a performance

e suggest ways in which the work might be improved.

Lesson Plan – 25 minutes

Theme:
Training class to listen, respond, concentrate and work together. The emphasis is on whole body movements and movements possible in isolated parts of the body. This total concentration on the teacher within whole class teaching is in contrast with most of their informal experiences at the start of infant school.

WARM-UP AND BODY TRAINING ACTIVITIES - 18 minutes

1 Begin by standing in a circle, hands joined, and able to see the teacher who sings and leads the class through the big actions.

Let's join hands in one big ring,
Let's join hands and let us sing,
Let's join hands, both high and low, (reaching up, then down)
Let's drop hands and wave 'Hello!' (repeat, with all singing)

2 What lovely singing and arm movements. Well done. Now put your hands together and stretch them right up to the ceiling – as big as a house.

3 Now, small as a mouse, bend down to touch the floor with your hands.

4 Move with me and say the words, please. Big as a house and small as a mouse. Big as a house – big stretch up on tip toes. Small as a mouse – knees bent, hands on the floor. Once again, say the words and do the actions for me, please.

5 Let's use our hands again. Clap and count with me. Clap, 2, 3, 4, 5, 6, 7, 8; clap, 2, 3, 4, 5, 6, 7, 8; 1, 2, 3, 4, 5, 6, 7, stop!

6 Let's all use our feet now, and go for a little walk, keeping in time with my drum beat. You can follow me if you like. 1, 2, 3, 4, 5, 6, 7, 8; walk, 2, 3, 4, 5, 6, 7, 8; march, 2, 3, 4, 5, 6, 7, stop!

7 That was very good and most of you stepped when the drum told you to. Some of you followed the drum and me, and some went walking by yourselves.

DANCE - Clapping and Stepping - 7 minutes

Let's make a little 'Clapping and Stepping' dance, and see if you can be brilliant, standing, clapping with me when the drum isn't beating, for eight counts, then marching about when the drum is sounding, for eight counts.

Ready . . . . begin! Stand and clap, stand and clap, 5, 6, 7, 8; march, march, with the drum, 5, 6, 7, 8; stand and clap, stand and clap, 5, 6, 7, 8; drum and steps, drum and steps, 5, 6, 7, 8.

Stop! That was excellent. Let's have a last practice and this time we'll make our clapping hands reach higher and higher, and we'll swing our arms smartly as we walk about. Ready . . . .

Finally, half the class watch the other half to experience the pleasure of performing and being praised and thanked, often with applause from observers.

LESSON NOTES AND NC GUIDANCE

Aids to ensuring that pupils behave, listen and respond well include:

a starting in a circle formation where all can see and be seen by the teacher.

b total concentration on the teacher and what is being said and done by the teacher. This concentration is essential after the informality and freedom while changing and getting ready for the lesson, and, possibly, during the previous lesson.

c specific, clearly understood instructions and images, and their repetition which the pupils enjoy.

d the security and understanding provided by the clear accompaniment by the teacher.

e the friendly 'togetherness' of a lesson with plenty of variety – action song, big body movements, clapping and marching to a drum.

f enthusiastic teaching with lots of encouragement and praise for equally enthusiastic participation and effort.

Lesson Plan – 25 minutes

Theme:
Focusing attention on the teacher, their bodies and the start/stop of the drum as they perform their movements together.

WARM-UP AND BODY TRAINING ACTIVITIES - 18 minutes

1 Begin with everyone sitting in a circle, spaced apart, and able to see and copy the teacher's actions and singing. Legs are straight out in front. Big arm movements as pupils touch named parts to accompany each line.

Heads and shoulders, knees and toes,
knees and toes, knees and toes,
Heads and shoulders, knees and toes,
we all clap hands together.

2 Well done. Lots of good actions and singing. Let's do it again with really high touches on top of the head and shoulders, and a big bend forwards to touch the knees and toes. Ready . . . . Heads and shoulders, knees and toes, knees and toes, knees and toes, Heads and shoulders, knees and toes, we all clap hands together.

   (Repeat with big arm swings sideways up to touch head and shoulders, and big forwards bends to touch knees and toes.)

3 Stand up now, please. Watch how I do tiny bounces with my feet just leaving the floor. Can you try it, letting your toes just leave the floor? Do it with me, like a ball bouncing low. Bounce, bounce, tiny bounce, 5, 6, once again; 1, 2, 3, 4, bouncing low, bouncing low; 1, 2, 3, 4, 5, 6, 7, stop!

4 Listen to the drum and do tiny running steps like a rolling ball, keeping in time with the drum. When the drum stops, be still and show me a small, rounded shape like a ball that uses your back and your arms. Ready . . . . go! Run, run, run, run, 5, 6, 7 and still!

5 What rounded shape have you made? Are you using your back and your arms to look like a little ball? Once again, with the drum, 1, 2, 3, 4, run, run, run and stop! Round and still, like a little ball, please.

6 Let's practise again. Show me your still, round, starting shape where you listen for the starting signal, the drum sounding. Run carefully, looking for good spaces, until the drum does a loud beat to stop you. Be still, and show me your best, little, rounded ball shape.

DANCE - The Little Ball - 7 minutes

We can call our dance 'The Little Ball'. Please stand, ready, in your own space. We will do eight little bounces like a ball. Then the drum sounds for us to run with tiny steps like a rolling ball. When the drum stops be still and show me your best, round ball shape. Ready . . . . bounce, bounce, 3, 4, 5, 6, now the drum; run, run, run, run, 5, 6, make a ball shape. Be still everybody so that I can see your round ball shapes. (Repeat two or three times.)

Well done again, everyone. Let's have half of the class sitting and looking at the other half. Look out for and tell me about good bounces, good running and nice round shapes.

LESSON NOTES AND NC GUIDANCE

Pupils should be taught to be physically active.

The appropriate physical activity for this young age group is inspired by teaching that includes:

a starting in a circle formation where all can easily see and focus on the teacher.

b specific exercises to develop body awareness by isolating individual parts and concentrating on them. 'Heads and shoulders, knees and toes . . . .'

c specific exercises to produce whole body movements, such as full stretches and bends, using joints and muscles to their limit for proper development.

d the use of song to focus attention, produce action and bring the class formally together at the start of the lesson. Song also develops language skills and vocabulary as pupils feel, at first hand, the meanings of words.

e repetition and clear accompaniment by the teacher.

f good use of imagery to communicate an idea. 'Little bounces, just like a ball bouncing low.' 'Be still and small in a round, ball shape'.

g enthusiastic, encouraging teaching by a teacher who gives the impression – 'This is fun.'

Lesson Plan – 25 minutes

Theme:
Body shape, which is an ever-present feature within our movement whether we are still or in motion. Still shapes that feel firm are physically demanding and need good body tension. Moving shapes should involve the whole body, particularly the spine.

WARM-UP ACTIVITIES - 4 minutes

1 All stand in a circle, spaced apart, and able to see and copy the teacher's actions as she or he recites the poem slowly.

My hands upon my head I place, on my shoulders, on my face;
On my hips I place them - so, then bend down to touch my toe;
Now I raise them up so high, make my fingers fairly fly,
Now I clap them, one, two, three, then I fold them silently.

2 Well done, everyone. Let's do those actions again. Hands are very clever, aren't they, as they touch and fly and clap. Ready . . . .

3 Our feet are also very clever. Show me the soft bounces we did last time, like a little ball (low, quiet, with a 'give' in the knees).

4 Now skip to visit all parts of the room. Swing your arms and legs up in front of you in your lively skipping.

MOVEMENT SKILLS TRAINING - 15 minutes

1 Sit down in your own space. Our bodies are all making a shape, different to everyone else's. I will say 'Hold . . . . Change.' 'Hold' means you sit very still in your shape. 'Change' means you show me a different shape. Ready? Hold . . . . change. Make a new shape. Hold . . . . change. Hold, feel your muscles . . . . change and hold.

2 This time you can sit or lie or stand or kneel to show me your interesting shapes. Ready . . . . hold . . . . and change. Hold, very still . . . . and change. Try a stretched shape with your muscles working hard.

3 Now try a bent shape. Use your arms, your back and your legs. Can anyone do a twisted shape or a nice, round, ball shape?

4 Keep doing your 'Hold!' and your 'Change!' on your own, without me saying it. I would like to see you try a funny shape or a robot shape or even an upside down shape. Keep working, please.

5 Thank you for all those brilliant, still shapes. Can you be very clever now and make whole body, travelling shapes as you tip toe or walk in and out of one another, without touching anyone?

6 You can twist to circle round someone; stretch arms in front to go through a little space; stretch arms sideways like an aeroplane to turn a corner; or curl, small, travelling slowly, like a little ball.

DANCE - Still and Moving Shapes - 6 minutes

1 Let's all do a still shapes and a moving shapes dance. Show me your best, still, starting shape. Feel your muscles.

2 Now travel with the tambourine beating, making your moving shapes, stretching, bending, wide or twisting, in and out of others and into spaces.

3 The loud bang means 'Hold!' your still shape until the tambourine starts asking you to travel again.

Continue to practise, and then half the class watch the other half.

LESSON NOTES AND NC GUIDANCE

Pupils should be taught to adopt the best possible posture and use of the body, using movements imaginatively as they travel, hold stillness and make shapes, for example.

Development of body shape awareness and understanding is helped by:

a starting in a circle formation where all can see and easily follow the teacher's actions with total concentration.

b starting with a poem to provide a focus for pupils' attention and actions.

c isolating and concentrating on individual body parts to feel the many, varied ways they can move

d giving clear, specific instructions. '"Hold" means you sit still in your shape. "Change" means you show me a different shape'.

e good use of imagery to clarify what is wanted – 'a ball shape; a robot shape; like an aeroplane; an upside down shape'.

f watching and learning from demonstrations by others, particularly when the demonstrations are accompanied by helpful comments from the teacher.

g enthusiastic, encouraging teaching by a teacher who always stands, sits and moves with good posture.

Lesson Plan – 25 minutes

Theme:
Space awareness and understanding that we can move in our own personal space and the whole room. We share the space so that we can all enjoy moving, unrestricted by others.

WARM-UP ACTIVITIES - 4 minutes

1 Find a nice, big space where you can move your arms without touching anyone. Pretend this space is a big bubble which you can push to make bigger.

2 Reach up high, on tip toes, with both hands and – push! Now, reach in front, to the sides, and even behind you – and push!

3 Who's good at balancing? Can you push to one side with your hands and push to the other side with a foot, at the same time?

4 With the music, let me see you leaving your bubble, and skipping and dancing to all parts of the room. When the music stops, get back inside your bubble.

(Repeat several times.)

MOVEMENT SKILLS TRAINING - 15 minutes

1 Stand in your own, big bubble. Show me how you can use different shapes to reach and push your bubble away. You can be long like a pencil, wide like a star, or you can twist to reach behind you.

2 Keep working, please, doing three or four different shapes, reaching to many parts of your own space. You can reach with hands and feet, sometimes using both at the same time.

3 Well done. I saw lots of big, strong shapes pushing bubbles out to make your own space grow. Now the music will help you to travel into the big space of the whole room. Off you go.

4 Stop. When the music starts this time, can you remember to visit all parts of the room – the sides, ends and the middle, never following anyone? Off you go.

5 Stop. Most of us are only using our feet as we travel, walking, running or skipping. Can you try some big, travelling shapes this time, like we did in our last lesson? Think about what your whole body looks like. I will be looking for stretched, wide, curled and twisted shapes. Go.

DANCE - Bubbles - 6 minutes

1 Find a partner who will stand next to you, in your shared bubble. Decide which one of you will be number one, and which number two. Hands up, number one . . . . Hands up, number two . . . . Good.

2 Number one, stay in the bubble, reaching to all the spaces above, to the sides and behind you, to make your own space bigger. Number two, travel with the music, visiting lots of room spaces and going round all the other bubbles. I will ask you to return to your partner and your own bubble again. When the music stops you and your partner will hold your best, still shape.

3 Well done, partners. Now we change over. Number two stays in the bubble, and number one goes travelling to the music. Remember – whole body shapes in your own space and in the big room space.

4 Let's try the whole dance twice through with a short stop after the first time. Show a good starting shape. Begin.

Half the class watch the other half to see good spacing, actions and firm shapes.

LESSON NOTES AND NC GUIDANCE

Pupils should be taught to be mindful of others and share space sensibly.

Being 'mindful of others' is best developed by including:

a an awareness of one's own personal space, including the parts we seldom reach – behind, out to the sides and high overhead, in addition to the well-frequented space in front.

b the recognition that having sufficient 'own space' is essential for satisfactory, safe, un-impeded physical activity.

c good use of imagery to clarify the extent of one's own surrounding space. 'Pretend the space is a big bubble'.

d an awareness of the whole room, shared space, and the desirable way to travel within it to ensure minimum interruption to others' movement. Pupils of all primary school ages will travel anti-clockwise in a big circle, impeding and being impeded by those immediately behind and in front of them unless taught to travel otherwise. 'Visit all parts of the room – the sides, ends and the middle, never following anyone'.

e praise for those trying hard to 'share the space sensibly and unselfishly'.

f activity with a partner to experience the fun and the pleasure of working with someone, planning interesting new activities that you cannot do on your own.

Lesson Plan – 25 minutes

Theme:
Travelling with neat footwork, varied actions and use of feet and legs as they walk, run, jump, skip, bounce, gallop and slide.

WARM-UP ACTIVITIES - 4 minutes

1 All stand in a big circle, ready to do some travelling actions. We will all sing the words and do the actions.

This is the way we walk to school, walk to school, walk to school,
This is the way we walk to school, on a cold and frosty morning.
This is the way we skip in the hall, skip in the hall, skip in the hall,
This is the way we skip in the hall, on a cold and frosty morning.
This is the way we run outside, run outside, run outside,
This is the way we run outside, on a cold and frosty morning.

2 That was very good. Let's do it again. Pretend it is a cold and frosty morning and we need to do lively actions to keep warm.

MOVEMENT SKILLS TRAINING - 15 minutes

1 I am going to follow the drum as it tells me what kind of actions to do. Would you like to follow it with me?

2 It says 'March like a soldier and swing your arms. Now tip toe with quiet, tiny steps, and arms not moving very much. Now skip and skip and swing your arms. Feet together, bounce along, 1, 2, 3, 4. Slide your foot along the floor, reaching forwards as you go. And gallop and gallop, 3, 4, lift your feet high off the floor. Run, run, run and jump; run, run, run and jump.'

3 Well done. That was good fun, following the drum leader. We need to practise again and try to space apart better. Pretend you each have a drum leader, looking for and taking you to good big spaces where you won't bump into anyone.

4 Show me a beautiful, ready to start, shape. I will tell you the actions. Keep in time with the drum. Marching . . . . Tip toe steps . . . . Skips . . . . Bounces . . . . Gallops . . . . Run and jump, run and jump, and stop! Show me your still, finishing shape.

DANCE - Follow the Drum - 6 minutes

1 For our dance, let's do 'Follow the Drum'. The drum will beat at different speeds with stops in-between the actions for you to show a strong, still shape, ready for the next action.

2 Listen for the drum, then start performing the action I tell you. When the drum stops, you stop. Show me a neat, still starting shape. Ready . . . . now! (Short, 10–12-second beat, followed by the louder beat which says 'Stop!' The still, held shape period before the next and different drum beat should be about four seconds, long enough for an infant to hold the shape.)

3 That was excellent. All sit down, listen to the drum and tell me what actions you think it is playing. (Hopefully, they will give correct answers – 'Galloping! . . . . Walking! . . . . Skipping! . . . . Sliding! . . . . Bouncing!' and be told 'Yes, well done.')

4 Stand up and show me your still, starting shape. This time I will not be telling you the different actions. Start and stop with the drum. Make your actions fit the sound each time.

LESSON NOTES AND NC GUIDANCE

Pupils should be taught to develop control, co-ordination, balance and poise in the basic actions of travelling and stillness.

The prime aim of all Physical Education lessons is to inspire vigorous, whole body, physically challenging activity. In addition to promoting normal, healthy growth we want our pupils to have well-controlled, neat, poised and versatile movement. These aims are assisted by:

a starting together in a circle, with a song focusing on some of the ways we can 'travel'.

b a lively teacher accompaniment, giving a picture of the right ways to walk, skip and run, with repetitions of the song to let pupils improve their performances.

c good fun, follow the leader, specific travelling actions which keep changing for variety and to hold pupils' attention.

d praise for, and demonstrations by, those whose actions are neat, quiet, well-controlled, and well-spaced.

e the attention-holding dance climax as pupils listen for and respond to the varying nature of the drumming.

Lesson Plan – 25 minutes

Theme:
Body parts awareness, learning to understand and 'feel' the ways in which the whole body and its isolated parts can move.

WARM-UP ACTIVITIES - 4 minutes

1 Stand where you can all see me, in your own big space. Do the actions of the song with me as I sing them slowly, and please help me with the singing.

Two little hands go clap, clap, clap,
Two little feet go tap, tap, tap,
Two little hands go bump, bump, bump,
Two little feet go jump, jump, jump,
One little body turns around,
One little child sits quietly down.

2 Well done. This time, can you show me how you can clap hands and bump hands high, or in front, or to one side of you, as if you were reaching out in a big bubble.

MOVEMENT SKILLS TRAINING - 15 minutes

1 Stand by yourself with lots of space around you. Show me a huge stretch, up to the ceiling. Now collapse like a rag doll with arms and head hanging down. Now draw big circles in front of you with both arms, one way round, then back the other way.

2 Let's be clever and join those three whole body movements together. Stretch up high to the ceiling; drop down like a rag doll; circle round with long arms; circle back the other way.

3 Excellent. One last practice and this time feel your whole body, arms, legs and back working as you move. Ready, begin . . . .

4 Let's try moving only one body part, starting with your shoulders. Lift them both, then lower. Lift one, then lower. Lift the other, then lower. Pull them forwards, push them back. Circle them forwards, up and back.

5 Arms next. Stretch them, reaching in many directions. Bend them in and stretch them out again. Arms can make big circles. They can punch firmly . . . . and shake loosely. Let them swing low from side to side.

6 Hands by themselves can clench and stretch; clap different parts of each other; come together slowly without a clap; explode apart quickly.

DANCE - Follow My Leader - 6 minutes

1 Find a partner and stand facing each other. Decide who is the leader and who will be the follower for our 'Follow My Leader' dance.

2 Leaders, you move, using one body part at a time, slowly, so that your partner can follow you easily. Use those parts we have already practised – shoulders, arms and hands, and do only two or three actions with each, so that you can repeat and remember them.

3 Half of the partners will take turns to perform for the other half. Look out for, and tell me about good actions you see in one body part only.

4 Thank you for your good, helpful demonstrations and comments. Next week, we will change over the leaders.

LESSON NOTES AND NC GUIDANCE

Pupils should be able to show that they can improve performance, alone and with a partner.

'Improvement' is assisted by:

a the lesson having a start, middle and end with an obvious unity of purpose and with pupils understanding what that purpose is. This lesson is all about concentrating on isolated body parts and using them neatly and to the limits of their possible movement

b bringing the class together at the start with a song with actions to practise, repeat, improve and develop. 'Can you do your handclaps high, or in front, or to one side?' (rather than only in front of you)

c specific coaching for quality, often with an accompanying demonstration, to clarify what is wanted. 'Show me a huge stretch, right up to the ceiling'

d the use of images to give a good picture of what is the ideal. 'Drop down like a rag doll.'

e specific coaching for variety by the teacher. 'Hands can clench, stretch, clap . . . .'

f partner work which necessitates thoughtful planning and decision-making when the leader, and provides new ideas when the follower

g learning from others' ideas during demonstrations.

Lesson Plan – 30 minutes

Theme:
Christmas.

WARM-UP ACTIVITIES - 4 minutes

1 Skip in your own space. Skip, skip, 3, 4, 5, 6, 7 and stop!

2 Clap hands in different spaces, high, low, in front or to one side. Clap, clap, 3, 4, clap, clap, 7 and 8. (Repeat skips and claps.)

3 Skip, travelling for six counts. On '7' and '8', face a partner to do gentle hand claps. Skip and travel, 3, 4, 5, 6, face a partner.

4 Clap hands with your partner for eight counts. Use one or both hands. Clap, clap, 3, 4, gently clap, skip again (. . . . and clap).

5 Brilliant! For the last four claps, you may say 'Happy Christmas when it comes!' Go! Skip, skip, 3, 4, 5, 6, find a partner; clap, clap, 3, 4, Happy Christmas, when it comes! Skip, skip . . . . Repeat.

MOVEMENT SKILLS TRAINING - 14 minutes

1 March, swinging your arms proudly to the tambourine beat. When it shakes, do a marching turn on the spot and then move off again.

2 March, march, 3, 4, swing your arms, now we turn; turn, turn, 3, 4, on the spot, then travel again. (Several repetitions for practice.)

3 Stand with body parts all loose and saggy, not like the firm body as we marched. Let head, shoulders and arms droop down in front of you. You feel as if you have no bones.

4 Now be slowly lifted up by an invisible string tied to your hands. Reach hands right up above your head. Oh! Someone has cut the string and you collapse down again. (Repeat the lift and drop.)

5 Lean forwards at the waist, with arms straight out sideways like wings. Show me how you can fly, glide, hover and zoom to different spaces. Remember to tilt your body to one side when you turn.

6 Lean forwards from your waist with one arm hanging forwards and one arm hanging behind. Show me your slow, heavy, elephant way of walking, and your trunk and your tail.

DANCE - Toy Factory · 12 minutes

1 In our 'Toy Factory' dance, the toy maker has had a very long and tiring day, getting all the toys ready for Christmas. He locks up and goes home. The toys, like young children, all love to move and play.

2 Let's all try to move like the toy soldier, marching, arms and legs swinging proudly, then turning on the spot.

3 Now, rag dolls, hang limp and loose until you feel the string pulling you up straight, then . . . . dropping you.

4 Aeroplanes, fly, rising and lowering; hover, sometimes on the spot; lean in to your turns at the corners; fly round one another.

5 Huge elephants, with heavy steps, reach forwards with your trunk and swish your tail behind.

6 Sit down and decide which toy you want to be – soldier, rag doll, aeroplane or elephant. Each group will dance by itself, then we can all work together until the toy maker comes back in the morning. We hear him opening the factory door and everyone has to go back to their places, be still and behave!

7 Get ready, soldiers. Go! . . . . Rag dolls . . . . Aeroplanes . . . . Elephants . . . . Now everybody, filling the toy shop with exciting action.

8 Rattle, rattle at the door. Back to places, still once more.

LESSON NOTES AND NC GUIDANCE

Pupils should be able to show control in linking actions together in ways that suit the activities.

We join notes to make music. We join words to make sentences. We join strokes of a brush, crayon or pencil to make art. We want our pupils to understand that they join actions to make 'movement'. The extent of the quality, variety and contrast within these 'joined up' actions determines the extent of the achievement and progress.

Developing control in linking actions together is assisted by:

a an easy to follow rhythm with sufficient repetitions of each of the two or three actions being joined. 'Skip and travel, 3, 4, 5, 6, 7, 8; clap, clap, 3, 4, clap, clap, 7, 8.'

b the teacher's vocal 'rhythm' accompanying the actions as a continual reminder of what is happening and what is about to happen. 'Skip and travel, 3, 4, 5, 6, face a partner; clap hands gently, 3, 4, clap, clap, now skip again; skip, skip . . . .'

c an interesting variety in each of the sets of two actions being linked, again assisted by the teacher's rhythmic reminders. 'March, march, 3, 4, swing our arms, now we turn; turn, turn, on the spot, 5, 6, march again.'

d the teacher understanding that a repeating pattern of two or three movements makes the pattern easy to remember, repeat and improve. 'Rag dolls hang all limp and loose; the strings now pull you tall and straight; rag dolls hang all limp and loose; the strings now pull you tall and straight.' 'Elephants slowly walk along; then they swish their trunk and tail; elephants slowly walk along; then they swish their trunk and tail.'

Lesson Plan – 25 minutes

Theme:
Simple, traditional style dance steps and figures.

WARM-UP ACTIVITIES - 5 minutes

1 Skip by yourself to visit every part of the room.

2 If your space is suddenly crowded, keep skipping on the spot, then travel on when there is plenty of room.

3 Skip for eight counts, join hands with a partner and dance for eight counts. Then you separate and dance by yourself for eight counts. Then you will join with a different partner for the next eight counts. I will be counting to keep us all together.

By yourself, 3, 4, 5, 6, join a partner. Hands joined, 3, 4, 5, 6, 7, split up. By yourself, 3, 4, 5, 6, find a new partner. Dance together, 3, 4, 5, 6, 7, split up. On your own, 3, 4, 5, 6, 7, 8.

TEACH STEPS AND FIGURES OF THE LESSON'S FOLK DANCE - 14 minutes

1 Listen to this country dance music. Let me hear you clapping your hands once to each bar of the music. I will count. You clap. Ready . . . . 1 . . . . 2 . . . . 3 . . . . 4; clap . . . . 2 . . . . 3 . . . . 4; clap . . . . clap . . . . clap . . . . clap. Well done. Most of you are feeling the rhythm of the music.

2 Now, let's see if you can skip in time with this lively music. Ready . . . . skip and skip and skip and skip, 1 and 2 and 3 and 4. (Several repetitions for practice.)

3 Join hands in a big circle. Let's practise all walking forwards together for four counts, then carefully walking backwards, back to our starting places.

4 One more practice, with the music this time. Can you help me, please, by counting out for four forwards and four back, so that we all keep together? Ready . . . . forwards, 2, 3, 4; back, 2, 3, again; in, 2, 3, 4; out, 2, 3 and stop. That was called 'Into the centre and out again' in country dancing.

Music   Any 32-bar English or Scottish country dance.

Formation   All stand in a circle with hands joined, and able to see and copy the teacher who is part of the circle.

Bars 1–8   All walk forwards into the centre for four counts, then all walk out backwards to your starting circle for four counts.

Bars 9–16   With hands by your sides, all skip forwards into the centre, then all skip back out to your starting places.

Bars 17–24   All bounce forwards into the circle, then bounce out again.

Bars 25–32   Join hands to make a big circle, all walk round, anti-clockwise, led by the teacher.

Repeat.

LESSON NOTES AND NC GUIDANCE

Pupils should be taught to perform movements or patterns, including some from existing dance traditions.

This welcome continuing requirement in the revised National Curriculum ensures a place for traditional as well as 'creative' dance for all primary school pupils. Both types of dance often have their enthusiasts and supporters in a typical staff room. Both can now be mutually supportive, sharing ideas and dances.

For beginners in folk dance, the teacher concentrates on:

a clapping to feel the timing of the music.

b teaching and practising the skipping travelling step by yourself and with a partner, using music that is quite brisk. The more expert the country dancer, the slower the music.

c rhythmically accompanying the groups of eight steps to each eight-bar phrase of the music. This keeps pupils in time with the music and gives reminders. 'Skip by yourself, 3, 4, 5, 6, find a partner; skip together, 3, 4, 5, 6, now by yourself'.

d circle dances with simple actions; pupils copy the teacher who joins in to demonstrate. At the simplest level, all the pupils perform throughout. These 'traditional style' simple dances introduce the class to some of the steps and figures of the established dances.

Lesson Plan – 25 minutes

Theme:
Variety in body part actions. Variety, like contrasts, adds interest for performers and observers.

WARM-UP ACTIVITIES - 4 minutes

1 Stand near a partner for our little dance. I will sing the words and I hope you will join in quickly, to help me.

See the little hands go clip, clip, clap,	(clap hands)
Then the feet go trip, trip, trap,	(stamp feet)
I've one word to say to you,	(point a finger)
Come shake hands, how do you do?	(partners shake hands)
Merrily we dance around, just so,	(skip round together)
Then we bow and off we go.	(bow, separate and find a new partner)

2 Well done, everybody. It is interesting to see the different hand and feet actions in that little dance. Let's all sing and dance again, and show me how different your actions can be.

MOVEMENT SKILLS TRAINING - 15 minutes

1 Sit down in a good space with your legs bent and feet flat on the floor. Lean back with your hands behind to support you. Try little steps on the spot. Step, step, step, step; step, step, step, stop!

2 Still sitting, walk feet forwards for four counts, then back for four. Forwards, 2, 3, 4; back, 2, 3, 4; walk forwards, 3, 4; back, 2, 3 and stop!

3 Jump up to standing. Do little, low jumps from one foot to the other. Jump, 2, 3, 4, foot to foot to foot to foot.

4 Stand with your feet apart. Can you swing from side to side, until your body is on one foot only each time with the other foot lifted off the floor? Swing, swing, side to side; 1, 2, 3 and still.

5 Remember where your own space is. Show me lively ways to travel away from and back to your own space. I will beat out eight counts to take you away, and eight counts to bring you back. Ready? Travel, travel, away, away, lively travel, 7, now back; travel back, travel back, 5, 6, home again.

6 Well done. Most of you managed that. Let's have one more practice and remember to do 'lively' skipping or running or bouncing.

DANCE - Clever Feet - 6 minutes

1 We'll call our dance 'Clever Feet' as we join together the actions we have just practised. All sit down and . . . . step on the spot, 3, 4; again on the spot, 3, 4; walk forwards, 3, 4; walk back, 3, 4.

2 Jump up and show me your low jumps from foot to foot. Jump, 2, 3, 4, foot to foot, 3, 4. Swing, swing, side to side; 1, 2, 3 and still.

3 Now the hardest part – trying to travel away for eight counts, then coming back to your place for eight counts. Ready? Go!

4 That was excellent. The sitting, the standing, the travelling and your very 'Clever Feet' made it interesting to look at.

5 Let's try to be very clever this time and do the dance straight through without stopping. My tambourine rhythm will help you. Get ready to start from a sitting position. Begin . . . . Standing . . . . Travelling . . . .

6 Let's have half the class performing and half enjoying watching some of the many actions our clever feet can do.

LESSON NOTES AND NC GUIDANCE

Pupils should be able to show that they can improve performance through practising their skills, applying them with co-ordination and control.

'Variety' can refer to a mixture of different actions being practised and improved, or a range of ways that one action can be performed. Variety is interesting and worthwhile for its own sake, and eventually is the biggest contributor to the class repertoire.

Improvement with the emphasis on variety is inspired by:

a direct teaching of specific skills by the teacher, as in the opening song.

b direct teaching of specific actions, as in the middle third of the lesson.

c indirect, shared choice teaching, as in the middle third of the lesson and the 'Clever Feet' dance, where pupils are challenged to plan 'lively ways to travel away from and back to your own space.' In shared choice teaching, the teacher decides the nature of the activity (travelling), and the pupils decide the actions.

d observing others demonstrating and then discussing any actions which they thought were special, worth remembering, worth copying – and, of course, praising.

Lesson Plan – 25 minutes

Theme:
Body contact sounds. Making and moving with the sounds.

WARM-UP ACTIVITIES - 4 minutes

1 Show me your favourite ways to travel to all parts of the room, listening to my drum beats. When the drum stops – suddenly sometimes – quickly show me a body shape that is still and without any wobbling. (Teacher continues playing and stopping, using different lengths of time for each action. The rhythm is varied to suggest skipping, marching, pattering, for example.)

2 Well done. You listened and moved really well. Watch this little group and see how they start and stop, exactly with the sounds.

MOVEMENT SKILLS TRAINING - 15 minutes

1 Can you make a sound with your hands? Try clapping your hands together for four counts, then slapping your hands against your legs for four. Go! Clap, clap, clap, clap; slap, slap, slap, slap; clap hands, 3, 4; slap legs, 3, 4. (Repeat several times for practice until everyone is feeling the rhythm.)

2 Very quietly, tap the floor gently, using each foot in turn. Tap, tap, tap, tap; tap, 2, 3, 4; change feet, change feet; 1, 2, 3, stop!

3 Now, can you show me four claps and four slaps, all accompanied by your quiet, gentle taps? Ready? Go! Clap and tap, clap and tap; slap and tap, slap and tap; clap, 2, 3, 4; slap, 2, 3, 4. (Repeat.)

4 Show me lively sounding stamps as you travel with firm steps, beating the floor. Stamp, stamp, 3, 4; swing your arms, lift your legs; beat, beat, beat the floor; firmly, firmly, 3, 4.

5 As you stamp forwards this time, can you make body sounds for me? You can clap hands or legs again, or you can make a new kind of sound. You can click fingers, clap a different body part with a hand (chest, shoulder, forearm; or slap upper arms against your sides). Keep your rhythm going with the drum. Stamp and travel, 3, 4; stamp and sound, 3, 4; strong legs, strong legs, keep going, keep going.

DANCE - Tapping and Stamping - 6 minutes

1 Let's do a 'Tapping and Stamping' dance. All start in your own space. Remember – feet keep tapping quietly as we clap hands for four, then slap legs for four. Let's try it three times through, and all make your sounds match my drumming. Go! Tap, tap, clap, clap; tap, tap, slap, slap; tapping and clapping, 3, 4; slapping and tapping, 3, 4. Repeat.

2 Excellent. Good sounds, good rhythm and very neat, gentle taps.

3 The second half of our dance has the stamping travelling accompanied by your choice of body sounds. Make both the stamping and your sounds big and lively, so they are different to the gentler, quieter tapping, clapping, slapping.

Ready? Go! Stamp and travel, making sounds; lively stamps and lively sounds; travel, travel to your sounds; stamping, sounding, stamping, sounding.

4 Well done. That looked much bigger than the smaller movements on the spot. Now we are going to put the two parts together – on the spot; then travelling. Tapping with clapping and slapping; then stamping with sounding. I will keep reminding you and help you with your rhythm. Show me your best starting shape. Begin!

5 Each half of the class will look at the other half. Look out for and tell me about good actions, good sounds, good rhythm.

LESSON NOTES AND NC GUIDANCE

Pupils should be taught to use rhythmic responses as they perform basic skills.

As they leave the hall after this lesson, one might expect the pupils to be chanting 'One, two, three, four; one, two, three, four' and stepping in time to their chant, after experiencing so many rhythmic practices led by the teacher and the drum – 'Clap, 2, 3, 4; slap, 2, 3, 4; clap and tap, 3, 4; slap and tap, 3, 4; stamp, stamp, 3, 4;' and so on.

Developing rhythmic responses is assisted by:

a listening to and responding to a rhythmic accompaniment such as a drum, often by standing or stepping; counting the four beats out loud and clapping in time with those beats.

b listening to and travelling to a rhythmic accompaniment, responding to its stopping and starting, and trying to respond in an appropriate way as the drum suggests marching, skipping, bouncing, sliding or galloping.

c making rhythmic sounds with hands or feet to a '1, 2, 3, 4', easy to feel, repeating beat.

d the teacher rhythmically accompanying the descriptions of the various actions, to help with the rhythm and to be a reminder of what is happening. 'On the spot, clap and tap; on the spot, slap and tap; travel and stamp, lively sounds; stamp and stamp, noisy stamps.'

Lesson Plan – 25 minutes

Theme:
Body contact sounds and rhythms.

WARM-UP ACTIVITIES - 4 minutes

1 Show me that you can 'feel' the rhythm of this lively country dance music by standing, tapping and clapping for eight counts; dancing away from me for eight counts; dancing back towards me for eight; then standing and stamping your feet for eight. Go! Stand and tap, stand and clap, 5, 6, now go away; dance away, 3, 4, travel, travel, now come back; dance back, 3, 4, 5, 6, stand and stamp; lift your knees, stamp, stamp, 5, 6, start again.

MOVEMENT SKILLS TRAINING - 15 minutes

1 All sit and see if you recognise the nursery rhyme I am sounding on the floor with my hands and my feet. Do not shout out the answer, please.

2 *'Humpty Dumpty sat on a wall'* sounded with both hands. *'Humpty Dumpty had a great fall'* sounded with soles of the feet. *'All the king's horses and all the king's men'* sounded with hands on the floor. *'Couldn't put Humpty together again'* using hands and feet.

3 When pupils identify the nursery rhyme, they remain seated and accompany the teacher in sounding it out on the floor, making their own sounds with hands and feet, and saying the words.

4 All stand and let us say the first line, making hand clapping sounds. *'Humpty Dumpty sat on a wall.'* You can tap if you like.

5 For the second line, dance and skip, making strong sounds with your feet, on the spot. *'Humpty Dumpty had a great fall.'*

6 For the third line, stand, clapping. *'All the king's horses and all the king's men.'* Tap, if you wish.

7 For the last line, dance about, making sounds with both hands and feet. *'Couldn't put Humpty together again.'*

8 Let's practise all four lines without stopping and let me hear your rhythms and your words loud and clear.

DANCE - Humpty Dumpty · 6 minutes

1 Find a partner and decide who is number one and who is number two.

2 Line one. Number one dances on the spot, making feet and handclapping sounds while two dances, circling round one, also making feet and handclapping sounds. *'Humpty Dumpty sat on a wall.'*

3 Line two. Change over and repeat, as for line one. *'Humpty Dumpty had a great fall.'*

4 Line three. They stand facing each other and carefully clap hands together to make the rhythm. *'All the king's horses and all the king's men.'*

5 For line four, they stand side by side, facing opposite ways and lean forwards to beat out the rhythm, very gently, on their partner's back. *'Couldn't put Humpty together again.'*

6 During our next practice try to keep both feet and hands working, without stopping.

Development can be through partners planning their own short body rhythms dance to a different nursery rhyme. Pairs can perform for other pairs to see if they recognise the new nursery rhyme.

LESSON NOTES AND NC GUIDANCE

Pupils should be able to improve performance, through practice, alone and with a partner.

The individual practice in the middle of the lesson is led by the teacher, who sets the rhythm and says the words of each line. The first and third lines can be accompanied with a handclap only, or with a responsive class, a handclap and a tapping of feet. Lines two and four are ideally accompanied by lively clapping and dancing on the spot, aiming to produce a strong and audible body sound accompaniment. Lines two and four are helped by a turning and circling to give the feet a little travelling to do.

When several practices have produced an obvious improvement, all take a partner to practise the partner version. Both should work non-stop, saying the words and accompanying them with hand and foot sounds for two lines, one on the spot, one circling; then facing to clap on line three; and finally, gently sounding the rhythm on each other's back on line four.

Once they are well-practised, they can be asked 'As I quietly say the words of the nursery rhyme, can you make clear body sounds to keep with me? If I close my eyes and say the words, would I feel and hear that you are accompanying me throughout? Then I will ask for volunteers to show the class their excellent actions and sound-making.'

Lesson Plan – 30 minutes

Theme:
Linking actions together in a controlled way. We want pupils to be aware of the actions, body parts, shapes and rhythms involved in these 'joined up' sequences.

WARM-UP ACTIVITIES - 5 minutes

1 Walk, 2, 3, 4 with low handclaps; four steps turning on the spot with high handclaps; four steps walking back to starting places with low handclaps; four steps turning with high handclaps. Step and clap, step and clap; turn and clap, turn and clap; step and clap low, step and clap low; turn and clap high, turn and clap high.

2 This time, let your walking steps be low and soft like your low, quiet handclaps. Let your turning steps be high and strong with high, strong handclaps. Quietly forwards, 3, 4; turn strongly, 3, 4; forwards, softly, 3, 4; stamp and turn, stamp and turn. Keep going.

MOVEMENT SKILLS TRAINING - 15 minutes

1 Like a bubble, can you float gently with your arms lifting high? Lift and float high . . . . turn, slowly and smoothly . . . . sink . . . .

2 Practise joining the parts smoothly. Float high in the air without a sound . . . . turn in the air, slowly round . . . . sink and lower, bending towards the floor.

3 Run, jump, land and be still, floppy like a rag doll. Keep it short and show me your floppy, still finishing shape. Run . . . . jump . . . . land . . . . and hold still, all loose and floppy.

4 Change from floppy to tall, ready to go again. Run, jump, land and be still.

DANCE - Joined Up Actions - 10 minutes

1 Stand beside a partner, facing different directions for our 'Joined Up Actions' dance.

2 Keep with the rhythm of the tambourine. Both partners will do the four quiet steps away from each other, with low handclaps; four strong steps turning with high handclaps; four steps back towards partner, clapping low; and four lively steps, turning, with high handclaps. Go!

3 Let's have another practice. Look at the floor to see where your starting place is – and try to be exactly there when you come together again. Ready . . . . step and clap, step and clap; turn and clap, turn and clap; back to partner, 3, 4; turning, turning, 3, 4.

4 We kept together there because of the tambourine. Let's now change to moving like a bubble, and I would like three of you to keep the rhythm by saying, 'Floating'; 'Turning'; 'Sinking'.

5 Sarah first, please. 'Floating'. Slowly, gently, up on tip toes.

6 Now Ian, please. 'Turning'. Smoothly, one way, then the other.

7 Now Jennifer, please. 'Sinking'. Lowering, very slowly, bending.

8 Well done dancers and speakers. You all worked hard to make it look smooth, neat and 'together'.

9 Now we can join the two very different parts together for interesting variety. Steps and claps, moving apart, then together. Then moving like bubbles, anywhere in the room.

10 In the next practice, feel what your hands and feet are doing in the stepping/clapping. Then feel inside your whole body as it floats, turns and sinks.

11 Half will now perform for the other half to watch and enjoy.

LESSON NOTES AND NC GUIDANCE

Pupils should be able to show control in linking actions together.

Planning and performing joined up actions neatly, with variety and contrast, is the mark of a good dancer or gymnast. A pupil's ability to work harder for longer at increasingly complex sequences of joined up actions eventually becomes the teacher's aim.

Successful control in linking actions together is assisted by:

a the teacher continually challenging the class to perform a series of actions, and repeat them, even in the warm-up part of the lesson with its 'Walk, walk, clapping low; turn, turn, clapping high; back to places, clapping low; turn, clap high, turn, clap high.'

b the use of imagery in a series of linked actions helps to give the flowing sequence interesting variety and contrast, as when the bubble 'floats . . . . turns . . . . sinks.'

c the teacher's vocal rhythmic accompaniment of the groups of actions to keep them flowing one after the other at the appropriate speed, and to ensure that actions are changed and not held too long.

d reminding pupils that we make 'movement' by changing and joining up actions in the same way that we join words to make sentences or join notes to make music.

Lesson Plan – 25 minutes

Theme:
Simple, traditional style dance steps and figures.

WARM-UP ACTIVITIES - 5 minutes

1 Skip by yourself, 'feeling' the eight-count pattern of this folk dance music. Can you change direction as you start a new count of eight? Skip, 2, 3, 4, 5, 6, change direction. Travel, 2, 3, 4, 5, 6, change again.

2 This time, skip quietly for six counts, then gently touch hands with someone coming towards you on '7' and '8'. Skip, 2, 3, 4, 5, 6, touch hands, touch hands. Skip, 2, 3, 4, 5, 6, meet and clap.

TEACH STEPS AND FIGURES OF THE LESSON'S FOLK DANCE - 14 minutes

1 Find a partner and stand side by side, holding hands, in a big circle, where you can all see me.

2 In 'advance and retire' we all skip forwards into the circle for four counts, then come out backwards for four counts. Ready . . . . forwards, 2, 3, 4; backwards, 2, 3 and stop. Two or three times without stopping, go!

3 In a chasse step, we face our partner, joining both hands, and step-close sideways, starting with the foot nearer the centre. Ready . . . . step-close, step-close, 3 and out again; step-close, step-close, step-close and stop.

4 Very well done. That is quite difficult. One more practice. Small steps, go!

5 All couples now stand side by side for promenade, hands joined, in an anti-clockwise circle. Keep in your big circle for our walk round in this direction. Go! Walk, 2, 3, 4, 5, 6, 7 and stop.

6 We need one more practice, just to get it perfect. Go!

7 Well done. We are all back in our starting places. Now give your partner both hands, and turn each other one way for four counts, then back the other way for four counts. Two hands turn, 3, 4; back again, 3, 4.

DANCE - The Muffin Man (English Folk Dance) - 6 minutes

Music   The Muffin Man or any 32-bar jig.

Formation   Big circle with partners.

Bars 1–8 All dance to the centre and back.
Bars 9–16 Face partner, taking both their hands and perform four chasse steps to the centre and back.

Bars 17–24   Promenade partners in an anti-clockwise direction.
Bars 25–32   Turn partners, four counts to one side, four counts back again.

Keep repeating.

LESSON NOTES AND NC GUIDANCE

Pupils should be taught to perform movements or patterns, including some from different times and cultures.

The 'showing control in linking actions' emphasis of the previous lesson is repeated here. Linking a series of actions together is an ever-present feature of folk dances, whether they are well-known existing dances or simple, traditional style dances created by the teacher and used to teach beginners some of the steps and patterns of traditional dance.

A four-part repeating pattern, with each part using eight bars of music of a 32-bar dance, is the most commonly used. For beginners to traditional dance the rhythm is quite quick and will have been practised and 'felt' in the warm-up activities.

Rhythmic accompaniment of the actions by the teacher is the best aid in learning to keep the rhythm. 'Skip, 2, 3, 4, 5, 6, change direction; travel, travel, 3, 4, 5, 6, change again.'

In learning the traditional dance of this lesson, the pupils can be carried along in time with the music, and reminded of the actions by the teacher's chanting of the instructions as he or she joins the class in performing them. 'Skip to the centre, 3, 4; skip back out again; chasse in, both hands joined, chasse back out again; side by side, we promenade round, 5, 6, 7, now turn; turn your partner, 3, 4, back, back, 7, 8 (keep repeating).'

Lesson Plan – 30 minutes

Theme:
Spring and growth.

WARM-UP ACTIVITIES - 5 minutes

1 Kneel down, curled very small. Stay kneeling, but let me see you start to grow. Unroll your back, shoulders and head, then your arms.

2 Once again, kneel and curl small, arms and head tucked in. Slowly, start to rise, bit by bit, and finish kneeling tall.

3 This time you choose which parts will reach up first. You might start with an elbow and one hand before moving any other part.

SPRING POEM AND MOVEMENT SKILLS PRACTICE - 16 minutes

1 Children, listen to this spring poem which is called *The Seed*.

In the heart of a seed, buried so deep,
A dear little plant lay fast asleep,
'Wake', said the sunshine, 'creep to the light',
'Wake', said the voice of the raindrops bright,
The little plant heard and rose to see,
How wonderful the outside world could be.

2 Curl up small, like a seed in the soil. I will read the poem. Show me how a seed might grow from being asleep.

3 This time, show me which part you are moving first as you start to grow. Head? Shoulders? Back? Elbow? Hand?

4 Decide this time if you want to stay kneeling, or if you are coming right up to standing, to have a better look at the world. You choose.

5 Our seed has grown and is looking at what it can see in springtime in our wonderful outside world. Can you tell me some of the things that are born in spring that you like?

6 Curl up small again and we'll try to show how a chicken pushes out from its egg, walks unsteadily and then steadily as it becomes stronger. Slowly, push against the inside of your egg. You can use your hand, elbow, shoulder, foot, knee, head or back. Please show me.

7 Now stand and show me how unsteady you might be for the first few wobbly steps – with some falling down included. Up and down.

8 Now you can run, jump and make a tiny flight.

9 Well done. Curl up small again and think about how a baby kitten might move soon after it is born. Keep curled, and roll on your back from side to side? Curl and roll. Curl up small and roll.

10 Lie on one side and do a great big stretch. Curl and roll on to your other side and stretch again. Curl, roll over, big stretch. Curl, roll over, big stretch. Well done. Good curls and stretches.

11 Jump up and land silently. Run, jump, turn and land silently. Run, jump with a turn and land silently. Curl up small and rest.

DANCE - Spring Dance - 9 minutes

1 For our dance, I will read out the seeds poem and your movements will accompany me. Then we will all show the movements of the very new, unsteady chicken and the curling, stretching, jumping kitten.

2 Feel your whole body movements this time as you grow; as you push out from your egg; as you do huge bends, stretches and rolls.

3 Practise; improve; remember; perform and observe; make comments.

LESSON NOTES AND NC GUIDANCE

Pupils should be taught to express and communicate ideas and feelings, responding imaginatively.

In Dance, feelings are always expressed through bodily movement. It is hoped that a class will be inspired to express inner feelings of pleasure, excitement, concentration, enthusiasm, etc., through their movement. If a mountaineer can claim to feel 'life effervescing within me' while on his beloved mountains, many young dancers can equally experience intense physical satisfaction.

The feelings we are seeking here is wonderment at springtime growth and new arrivals coming into the world. The purely physical feelings of parts stirring, pushing, appearing and growing is accompanied by feelings of coming alive, of 'being', of release and relief and wanting to have a first look at what the world is like.

There is wonderment at nature as the tiny plant, the chicken and the kitten all manage, unaided, to come alive. The clever plant looks up at the sun; the clever chicken manages, after initial wobbling, to walk, run, jump and do a short flight; the clever kitten learns quickly to do many body movements as well as running, jumping and landing beautifully and softly. Nature is wonderful.

Lesson Plan – 30 minutes

Theme:
Fast and slow movements as one example of interesting and sometimes exciting contrasts.

WARM-UP ACTIVITIES - 5 minutes

1 Remind yourselves of some of the ways you can travel to a lively piece of music. Show me your best travelling. Go!

2 Hands up all those who were skipping . . . . running . . . . walking . . . . bouncing . . . . hopping . . . . pattering . . . . sliding, etc.

3 Clap with me to the music and feel how easy it is to do groups of four claps. 1, 2, 3, 4; clap, clap, clap, clap; 1, 2, 3, 4; 1, 2, 3, stop!

4 Travel any way you like for four counts, then stay in your space and do four movements (e.g. steps; knee bounces; jumps; bounces; turns; handclaps; whole body shakes). Travel, 2, 3, 4; stay and move, 3, 4; off you go, 3, 4; on the spot, 3, 4. (Repeat, several times.)

MOVEMENT SKILLS TRAINING - 15 minutes

1 Stand in your own big space and show me a shape that tells me how you are going to move suddenly and very fast. Get ready. Go, go, go, fast; quick, 2, 3, 4; rush, rush, rush, be still!

2 Travel again, fast, using all your muscles – go! Quick, quick, quick, quick; go, go, go, go; 1, 2, 3, fast; quick, quick, quick, stop!

3 Try your fastest possible movements in your own space this time. Move, move, move, fast; quick, quick, 3, 4; 1, 2, 3 and stop!

4 That was very fast, tiring and hard work. Now show me how slowly you can travel. Start in a shape that tells me what you will be doing. This will be your slowest-ever moving. Begin.

5 That was v-e-e-ry s-s-l-ow! Well done, everybody. You can change level if you wish and r-o-ll or cr-aw-l, as well as your slow travel on your feet. Ready . . . . slowest-ever . . . . go.

6 In your own space, do slow movements using your whole body in bends, stretches and twists as well as slow-motion steps, knee bends and stretches, on the spot.

DANCE - Fast and Slow - 10 minutes

1 Surprise me with your sudden, fastest-ever and slowest-ever movements. You can travel or perform in your own floor space. Go!

2 You decide when to change from high speed to almost no speed. We should have an exciting mixture of speeds happening at the same time because you are all changing speeds at different times.

3 Your dance will be more interesting if you do: fast moves, travelling; slow moves on the spot; fast moves on the spot; slow moves travelling, for example.

4 Find a partner and number yourselves one and two. Number one will dance and two will watch to look for any special ideas that can be shared with the rest of us. Number one, begin.

5 Thank you, number ones. Number twos, do any of you want to tell us about something you particularly liked in your partner's 'Fast and Slow' dance? (Comments; observation; further comments and thanks.)

6 Change places, please, and let's have number two ready to show off their dance. Number ones, watch your partner's actions and good ideas to share them with us.

7 Further practice allows good ideas to be used by everyone.

LESSON NOTES AND NC GUIDANCE

Pupils should be taught to develop control and balance in the basic actions of travelling, jumping, turning and stillness.

The 'control' referred to here is speed control, to show high speed or slow motion and travelling actions from place to place, cleverly adapting the size of the steps to keep balanced and in control of the whole body.

Ultra-high speed and slow motion whole body movements on the spot include actions such as bending, stretching, twisting, turning and arching, and leg actions that can be performed on the spot, such as jumping, running, bouncing and stepping.

Bursts of fast travelling or body movements on the spot should be short because they are so intense, 'using all your muscles.' Ultra-slow travelling can be performed at floor level, with log rolling by a stretched body, or sideways roll with a curled up body. Ultra-slow movement on the spot will invite reaching out to all the spaces around you, to the front, sides, high above and behind as well as pulling back into oneself, bending and stretching legs and spine.

A good test of pupils' control is for the teacher to call 'Stop!' suddenly and see how quickly they 'freeze' into stillness.

Lesson Plan – 30 minutes

Theme:
Summer holidays.

WARM-UP ACTIVITIES - 4 minutes

Stand in a circle, hands joined and able to see the teacher who sings and leads the class through the big actions.

Let's join hands in one big ring,
Let's join hands and let us sing,
Let's join hands, both high and low, (reaching up, then down)
Let's drop hands and wave 'Hello!' (repeat, with all singing)

MOVEMENT SKILLS TRAINING - 16 minutes

1 Listen to this music. It is called *Those Magnificent Men In Their Flying Machines*. Their aeroplanes were small, but they could turn, go up and down, slow down and speed up quite easily.

2 All get ready for take-off in your own little magnificent machine. Show me your beautifully stretched wings. Go!

3 Fly to every part of the room, weaving in and out of other aeroplanes. Keep your streamlined shape and let me see you leaning to one side as you do a sharp turn.

4 Well done. I saw some excellent weaving in and out, skimming past lots of other wing tips.

5 When I stop the music next time, you will show me with your movements some of the things that might be happening down below you. Flying, with lots of gliding and soaring, go!

6 Stop! Show me what might be happening at the seaside (swimming, floating, paddling, rowing, diving, building a huge sandcastle).

7 That was a good mixture. Well done. Now we fly again.

8 Stop! Show me what big, lively actions can happen in a children's playground (climbing frames, swinging, see-saw, skipping, throwing and catching, cycling, jogging).

9 What a brilliant playground with something interesting for everyone. That was very good. Back to flying again.

10 Stop! We are over a big zoo, now. Please show me with your actions and body shapes which animals are in the zoo (monkeys, elephants, penguins, dolphins, seals).

DANCE - Summer Holidays - 10 minutes

Music   From *Salute to Heroes* by Central Band of the R.A.F.

1 Let's put all the parts of our 'Summer Holidays' dance together now. Our aeroplanes are like magic carpets taking us to see some of the places children visit during their holidays.

2 All ready for take-off in your magnificent machines? When the music stops I will remind you of where you are. Off you go.

3 Seaside – swimmers, floaters, rowers, divers, sandcastle makers.

4 Flying. Show me your gliding, ups and downs, and your turns.

5 Children's playground – climbing, swinging, skipping, throwing and catching, cycling, jogging.

6 Flying, weaving in and out, looking down for the zoo.

7 Zoo – monkeys, elephants, penguins, dolphins, seals.

8 Really well done. I enjoyed seeing all those different holiday actions. Let's have another practice, then show one another.

LESSON NOTES AND NC GUIDANCE

Pupils should be taught to perform simple movement patterns.

One dictionary defines 'Pattern' as 'an arrangement of repeated parts'. Improved performance comes from practising, repeating, and remembering a manageable sequence of two, three or more simple actions. Without such repetition there will be no week by week development or improvement.

While *Those Magnificent Men In Their Flying Machines* may zoom around freely, sharing the whole room space, vigorously twisting, turning, weaving and gliding in and out of one another, as soon as they are challenged to represent the actions taking place down on the ground we want two things – whole body, vigorous actions, joined in such a way that they can be remembered, repeated, improved, and, of course, enjoyed and demonstrated.

For example, at the seaside – 'Swim forwards, swim forwards; float going backwards.' In the playground – 'Sit still on swing; swing forwards; swing back; swing forwards and back to sitting.' At the zoo – 'Elephants, stand on hind legs (lift head and arms forwards and up high in front, as if standing on rear legs); walk forwards, 3, 4 (upper body and arms dangling down in front of you).' Keep repeating the sequence of joined up actions.

Lesson Plan – 25 minutes

Theme:
Space and body shape awareness; controlled and rhythmic travelling and stopping in a quiet, responsive and co-operative environment.

WARM-UP ACTIVITIES - 4 minutes

1 All stand in a big circle, where we can see one another, with your feet apart for balance. Let us make circles with different body parts. Circle one shoulder forwards and back three times, then the other shoulder.

2 Bend one arm and circle your elbow forwards, up, and behind three times, then do the same with the other one.

3 Circle one long arm forwards, up, and behind three times, then the other long arm.

4 Let's do those three sets of circling again and try to make the circles even bigger by using your legs and body more, and reaching to spaces in the front and at the rear. Shoulder . . . . elbow . . . . arm.

MOVEMENT SKILLS TRAINING - 13 minutes

1 Somewhere in the room is an empty space for you to find and visit. Can you see it? Ready. Skip straight to it, pause, and show me a clear, big body shape. Go! Can your shape use a lot of space? Reach out far and spread yourselves. Keep still.

2 Look for your next empty space. Creep to it and freeze into the smallest possible shape. Go! How is your body supported? On feet, knees, back or side? Are you using only a tiny amount of space?

3 Look around again for your next, near space. Run and jump into it and use lots of space for your big, wide body shape. Go!

4 Tip toe to your next space and melt into the smallest shape. Go! Who is the tiniest, most curled-shape person?

DANCE - Going and Stopping - 8 minutes

1 In our 'Going and Stopping' dance, show me your best starting shape which might show me what your first, lively travelling action will be. Then travel to a space and stop in the biggest shape you can make. Go!

2 Be still. Feel your body working hard to fill the space.

3 Look for your next space. Travel to it with a gentler action, like walking, sliding, gliding, creeping and show me your tiny shape, using hardly any of the space. Go!

4 Be still and tiny, whether on feet, knees, back, side or upended on your shoulders.

5 Relax and rest for a moment. Well done, travellers and shape makers.

6 From now on you will decide when to move on to your next space without a signal from me. It would be brilliant if you were able to do this in a nice, rhythmic way, saying to yourself 'I travel, travel, travel, then make a huge shape; I move, move, move and hold a small shape; I go, go, go and hold my best shape.' Begin.

7 What excellent large and tiny shapes! I like watching your varied travelling – some lively and some more gentle – and I like your varied shapes – the biggest possible and the tiniest possible. Keep working hard to show me the differences.

8 Half the class will watch the other half. Watchers, please look for and tell me about big and small shapes, neat travelling, and any rhythmic actions.

LESSON NOTES AND NC GUIDANCE

Pupils should be taught to:

a *respond readily to instructions.* Direct teaching of specific activities in the warm-up should be accompanied by the whole class being seen to be active and responding. Direct teaching in the middle part of the lesson necessitates their listening carefully to the varied challenges. Anyone not listening is soon discovered. An enjoyable lesson with a variety of interesting material, taught and demonstrated by an enthusiastic and encouraging teacher, is the best incentive to equally enthusiastic participation.

b *be physically active.* The onus is on the teacher to 'get on with it', with the minimum of long-winded explanations. 'Creep to your next space and freeze small. Go!' While there is a lot of freedom in the 'Going and Stopping' dance, the pace is dominated by the teacher moving pupils on from stage to stage – keeping them listening, attending, planning and responding.

c *be aware of the safety risks of inappropriate clothing, footwear and jewellery.* September is the time to lay down essential traditions for the way the new class dress, behave and respond in Physical Education lessons.

Lesson Plan – 25 minutes

Theme:
Body parts awareness.

WARM-UP ACTIVITIES - 5 minutes

1 Find a big space where you can see me and move without touching anyone. Put your feet apart for good balance and reach high with both arms. Bend your arms, neck, back, waist, knees and ankles until you are crouched down with your hands on the floor. Now, stretch up your ankles, knees, waist, back, neck and shoulders and finish with your arms high above your head again. (Repeat several times, bending, stretching and thinking about the joints concerned.)

2 Let's move round now, singing and making these actions together.

If you're happy and you know it, clap your hands,
If you're happy and you know it, clap your hands,
If you're happy and you know it, and you really want to show it,
If you're happy and you know it, clap your hands.
If you're happy and you know it, stamp your feet,
. . . . bend your knees . . . . wave your arms . . . . shake all over.

MOVEMENT SKILLS TRAINING - 12 minutes

1 Show me some happy travelling actions to visit all parts of the the room.

2 Stop a minute and look at these four happy travellers and their skipping, galloping, bouncing, running and jumping.

3 Find a partner for 'Follow My Leader' with each of you showing the other your happy travelling actions. You might use some of the good ideas we have just seen. Watch your partner's feet, legs and whole body and try to copy and follow. Change leader when I call 'Change!' Off you go.

4 Now, stand facing your partner. Show me these friendly hand actions. Wave one hand; wave the other hand; clap both hands, gently, 1, 2, 3, 4, starting high and coming down, down, down to just in front of you both. Wave, wave; clap, clap, clap, clap.

5 Let's keep a nice, slow rhythm this time – wave, wave; clap 2, 3, 4; high wave, high wave; high claps, both hands, lower and lower. Friendly wave and wave; friendly claps, claps, claps, stop!

DANCE - Follow My Leader - 8 minutes

1 Partners, stand ready, one behind the other. When I call 'Travel!' the leader will show his or her lively, happy travelling for the partner to copy. When I call 'Stop!' partners face each other, ready to wave and clap. Let's take it to there. Travel! . . . . Stop!

2 Try not to lose your partner by rushing ahead too far. Show your partner neat feet and leg actions to copy. Stand, ready, now for the other one to lead when I call 'Travel!'

3 Travel! Look for spaces, leaders, please, and keep repeating your one or two actions.

4 Stop! Face each other and show me your waves and your handclaps at a nice, slow speed – wave, wave; clap, clap, clap and stop!

5 Well done, new leaders and followers. In our next practice you will decide when to change from travelling to waving and clapping and when to start travelling again. All ready? Begin.

6 First leader leading; stop and face each other; other leader leading.

LESSON NOTES AND NC GUIDANCE

Improvement comes with thoughtful, focused practice and repetition of, ideally, rhythmic movement. Good practice for this is the warm-up activity with its repeating, rhythmic movements keeping everyone together with the teacher.

In 'Follow My Leader' we want the leader to be aware of the two or three repeating, travelling actions being performed so that they can be remembered, repeated and improved.

The teacher-directed 'Wave, wave; clap, 2, 3, 4; high wave, high wave; slow claps, 2, 3, 4' means that pupils do not have to remember this as well as their travelling. All can be kept together and reinforced as the teacher rhythmically accompanies the actions.

Another incentive to focused, thoughtful planning and improving is the tradition of presenting half of the class to the other half in a demonstration followed by comments. All then know that they will be looked at.

Lesson Plan – 25 minutes

Theme:
Autumn.

WARM-UP ACTIVITIES - 5 minutes

1 Our dance is going to be about 'Autumn Leaves'. Show me any kind of flying actions to visit all parts of the room.

2 Stay where you are, just like a helicopter, hovering, gently up and down, lifting and turning and floating. Good.

3 Glide straight across the room. Tilt over to one side to turn. Glide, zoom straight, turn with a lean, and let one wing go higher than the other. Good. You all look beautifully streamlined.

4 Fly like a glider, going down, down at speed and then up. This is called 'soaring'. Keep your wide wings shape. Soar down and up.

5 Well done, flyers. All come in to land now, please, and look at what I collected last night.

MOVEMENT SKILLS TRAINING - 12 minutes

1 These fallen leaves have all flown down from their trees in the last few days. Watch what happens when I throw one in the air.

2 What did it do? Yes, it floated, twisted down – but not in a straight line. It even seemed to hang in the air at one point.

3 Still sitting, lift your hands up high and let me see your fingers gently falling to the floor, twisting, turning, hanging, then falling without a sound, like a leaf.

4 Change to kneeling to give your leaf a higher start and to let you do a bigger body move in front, to one side, or even behind you. Let your fingers start in a shape of one of my leaves that you like. Are you crinkly, wide, flat, long, twisted or jagged? Surprise me with their interesting flying movements and shapes.

5 Start the movement very high, standing on tip toes, almost as high as some of the trees where the leaves started. As your fingers drift, float, twist and turn, falling, your whole body will need to lower, settle and try to melt into the floor, very carefully with no bumps. Practise a few times, gently.

6 All stand and let me hear you making a gentle wind noise to start your leaf fluttering. The wind gets stronger and louder and you fly off into space, twisting, turning, hovering, gliding.

7 The wind noise dies away and your leaf slowly falls to the ground, rolling over, two or three times. Is your body shape the same as your hands were at the start?

DANCE - Autumn Leaves - 8 minutes

1 Half of the class sit down round the outside of the room, ready to make sounds as they blow, like the wind, gently, strongly, then gently. The other half prepare to float up and down; then snap away into space, flying, gliding, soaring; then settling to land and roll along the ground to rest and show their final shape.

2 Change places. Wind makers, a gentle light wind to start, please.

3 Now, it's a very stormy, loud wind. Leaves make big, disturbed movements, then the storm passes, the wind sound softens and the leaves fall gently, rolling over and over on the ground. If you are an unusual-shaped leaf, I might pick you up to show you off!

4 One more turn each, then we can discuss any performances that we particularly enjoyed, and try to explain why we liked them.

LESSON NOTES AND NC GUIDANCE

Pupils should be taught to use contrasts of speed, shape, direction and level.

Speed Observing a leaf falling from a height, or imagining it falling from a high tree, will inspire descriptive words such as 'floating; turning; hovering; gliding; soaring; swooping; dropping; falling', all of which provide practice in using contrasts of speed.

Shape Observing a group of leaves brought into class will inspire descriptive words such as 'curly; flat; crinkly; wide; long; twisted; jagged' and will provide excellent images for the body to practise and feel.

Direction and level Leaves glide straight ahead; drop and then soar to a higher level; are buffeted from side to side by the wind; hang momentarily, then are blown backwards to where they came from, before dropping down, down to the ground.

Leaves provide excellent images because they are so common and because of the variety of interesting ways in which they move.

Lesson Plan – 25 minutes

Theme:
Sounds that inspire and accompany actions.

WARM-UP ACTIVITIES - 5 minutes

1 Cross your arms so that your hands rest on the opposite shoulder. Take slow, giant, noisy strides and slap your shoulders loudly. Slow, loud, giant strides; 1, 2, 3, 4; slow, slow, 3 and stop!

2 Now, something completely different. Up on tip toes for tiny, fast, pitter-patter steps. Hands quickly and gently slap sides of thighs. Fast – go! Step, step, step, step, 5, 6, 7, 8; quick, quick, quick, quick, 5, 6, 7, 8; slap legs, slap legs, 5, 6, 7, 8. That was fast! Good.

3 Find a partner and stand one behind the other. Try the giant, slow strides with claps and the tiny, fast steps with slaps. Leaders, ready? Go! Slow, slow, slow, slow; quick, 2, 3, 4, 5, 6, 7, 8; slow, slow, loud steps; quick, quick, quiet steps, 5, 6, 7, 8. Well done. Change places and show me the different actions and sounds.

MOVEMENT SKILLS TRAINING - 12 minutes

1 With me, all say the words on my card. Listen to how they sound different to each other.

SIZZLE! Show me how something might move if it's sizzling. Say it again. What does it make you think of? (Fuse of a firework; sausages frying.)
ZOOM! What sort of action will this be? Slow or quick? Gentle or lively? What could it be? (Rocket; motorbike.)
WHOOSH! This sounds a bit like the wind sounds we made last month, doesn't it? In addition to the wind, what might it be? (Firework at the top of its flight, opening out.)
BANG! What sort of action would 'Bang' be? (Firework exploding, scattering into space; a car crash.)

2 Practise moving to these words and saying them. Try to show me the speed and the force you feel is right for each word.

3 If you see pictures in your head as you do the actions, that will help you to make the movement more 'real'.

4 Have a last practice. Put your whole voice into the words and your whole body into the actions.

DANCE - Sizzle! Zoom! Whoosh! Bang! - 8 minutes

1 Those were very exciting sounds and actions. Can we look first at all those whose sounds have been used to accompany fireworks – probably a rocket. Show the sizzling fuse; the zooming start; the whooshing up into space; and the big bang explosion, with all the scattering of parts. Go! (Watch; comment.)

2 Well done. I hope any real rockets you see will be as splendid as yours. Now, let's have a look at the others whose actions were used to show something other than fireworks. We will watch them carefully and guess what they are showing us. (Watch; guess; make helpful comments.)

3 All keep practising your exciting actions with your own sound. Show me clear actions, good shapes and speed and a good finish.

LESSON NOTES AND NC GUIDANCE

Physical Education should involve pupils in planning.

Following the introductory class discussion about the nature of the four words and what sort of actions they might inspire, the imaginative planning of ways to use, co-ordinate and express the words in action begins.

Good use of the elements emphasised in the previous lesson – contrasts of speed, shape, direction and level – will enhance the quality, variety and contrast of the eventual performance.

Positive personal qualities such as enthusiasm, imagination and willingness to work hard at a challenge are evident in some of the outstanding planning that takes place, as is a willingness to listen to and adapt to the views of a partner.

While most demonstrations display good ideas for neat, controlled, versatile movement which had to be planned, demonstrations in this lesson also display highly individual, surprising and exciting ideas for others to see and try.

Lesson Plan – 25 minutes

Theme:
Simple, traditional dance steps and figures.

WARM-UP ACTIVITIES - 5 minutes

1 Listen to this country dance music and count out its rhythm with me. 1, 2, 3, 4, 5, 6, 7, 8. This time, clap and count with me.

2 Skip to the music and see if your clapping is still keeping in time with the music. Skip, 2, 3, 4, clapping, clapping, 7, 8. Keep going, 3, 4, clap and skip, 7 and stop!

3 I am going to divide the class into ones and twos. Number ones, you will skip in and out of the twos who are standing still. Do this for eight of my counts and then we change over. Ready, ones? Go! Number ones skip, 3, 4, round the twos, 7, 8; twos skip all around, 5, 6, 7, 8; ones again, 3, 4, skip, skip, 7, 8; twos go, 3, 4, skipping, skipping, 7, 8. (Demonstrate with dancers whose movements are neat, quiet and in time with the music. Class practice then allows all to try out some of the good ideas seen.)

TEACH STEPS AND FIGURES OF THE LESSON'S FOLK DANCE - 14 minutes

1 All the number ones stand in a long line down this side, please. Raise your arms sideways to keep you away from the person standing next to you. You need lots of space in your line.

2 All the number twos stand in a line facing the ones and you will be opposite a partner, about two big steps apart. We are all now standing in what is called a long set in country dancing.

3 Country dancing is very friendly, so step forwards and say 'Hello!' to your partner. Then step back into your long, straight line. Once again, forwards, 'Hello!' and back again.

4 Number twos, stand still, because ones are going to walk round in front of you, and back to their own places. There's no hurry, ones. You have eight counts to do it. Ready? Walk in front of partner, 3, 4, back to own line, 7, 8.

Good. Nearly everyone got there. Again ones to make it perfect. 1, 2, round in front of partner, cross back, 7, 8.

5 That was brilliant. Number twos, you have seen it done twice. Your turn now. Go round in front of partner, back to place, 7, 8. Again. Number twos travel, 3, 4, round, across, and back to own place. Well done.

6 Join both hands with your partner. All face the platform end of the room where the music is. We are going to skip for four counts, then, with hands still joined, turn and skip back to your own places. Ready. . . . skip forwards, 3 and turn; skip back into your places. Once again, join hands . . . . skip, 2, 3, turn; skip back to your places.

DANCE - Long Set With Partners- 6 minutes

Music Any lively, 32-bar English or Scottish dance tune.

Formation One long set, partners about two metres apart.

Bars 1–8 Both advance, shake hands, say 'Hello!' and go back to your own places.

Bars 9–16 Ones dance round in front of twos and back to places.

Bars 17–24 Twos repeat round in front of partners and back.

Bars 25–32 Partners join hands, face the top of the set, and skip forwards for four; turn and skip back to places for four. Repeat.

LESSON NOTES AND NC GUIDANCE

Pupils should be taught to be physically active and to gain positive attitudes to being active.

Folk dance lessons are among the most physically demanding. The steps are lively and we can practise and repeat them, without stopping, for several groups of the eight-bar phrases of music typical of most English and Scottish folk dances.

The simple figures, involving one couple, are easy to teach after a brief demonstration and explanation, and for most of this dance everyone is involved non-stop. As before, vocal rhythmic accompaniment of the actions keep the whole class working together. 'Ones in front of twos, back to your own place; twos in front of ones, back to your starting place.'

The 'planning' that was emphasised in the previous lesson is equivalent to the thinking ahead here, to be doing the right things at the right times, particularly if the teacher stops his or her accompaniment to check if the class can remember the different parts of the dance.

Lesson Plan – 25 minutes

Theme:
Christmas

WARM-UP ACTIVITIES - 4 minutes

1 All crouch down in a big space, well away from everyone. Listen to my poem and join in the actions:

Jack in the box jumps up like this,
Makes me laugh as he waggles his head,
I gently press him down again,
Saying 'Get in the box! You must go to bed!'

2 Help me with the words this time, please, as you do the actions. Show me the difference between the sudden, quick spring up and the slow squeeze down again, What funny waggling of your head will you do to make me laugh? Ready? *'Jack in the box jumps up . . . .'* (Demonstrate good examples of quick and slow contrasts.)

MOVEMENT SKILLS TRAINING - 13 minutes

1 Stand tall and proud like a fairy on a small platform. Show me how you will turn on the spot with tiny steps, like a dancer.

2 One hand will hold your magic wand and the other arm is used to balance as you take your tiny, tip toes, turning steps.

3 As you turn, your arms can go up and down. If I count to four, try to do one complete turn. Tip toes turning for 1, 2, 3 and 4. Now, back the other way, tip toes turning, 3, 4.

4 Let's all stand, floppy, like a circus clown, then jump up like a jack in the box. Try a funny walk, staggering forwards, back, side to side, throwing your arms in the air. Then pretend to throw a pail of water at someone. Stagger forwards, back, side to side, throw water.

5 Stiffen up now robots, swinging your long straight arms and legs and doing sudden changes of direction. 1, 2, 3, quick spin turn. Keep your head looking straight ahead. If you want to see to one side, turn your whole body to face that way. Walk, walk, walk, turn.

6 Penguins, keep your flippers down at your sides, making small swimming movements. Walk tall, but lean from side to side as you go. Waddle, waddle, waddle, flippers, flippers, flippers.

1 Steve, will you come to the middle and dance as the fairy who is going to do a complete turn, then point the wand to make a group come alive. The next turn and point by the fairy stops that group. Let's all dance as clowns, then robots, then penguins, being started and stopped by Steve's magic wand. Steve, please begin. (A pattern for each group is encouraged. Clowns spring up; stagger forwards, back, side to side; throw water. Robots, forwards, forwards, spin; forwards, forwards, spin; forwards, forwards, spin. Penguins, waddle, waddle, waddle, flippers, flippers, flippers.)

2 Thank you Steve, and well done all you toys. Sarah, will you be the fairy, starting and stopping each of the three separate groups I have now organised. Clowns, then robots, and then penguins, keep an eye on Sarah for your start and stop signals. When you are not dancing, watch the dancing group and tell me about any brilliant ideas you have seen.

LESSON NOTES AND NC GUIDANCE

Pupils should be able to show that they can show control in linking actions together in ways that suit the activities.

Being able to plan simple skills and perform them as joined up actions, neatly and with control, is the main requirement of the National Curriculum. Endlessly doing the same action, either on the spot or as a way to travel, is as inappropriate and pointless as writing one word or playing one note would be. From the very earliest stage, pupils should have been made aware that a sequence or pattern of movement requires at least two joined up actions.

When the two or more actions being practised show variety and contrast, the teacher should be heard identifying the good things seen. 'Well done, Susan. Your floppy clown looked like it had no bones or muscles. Your sudden spring up surprised me with lots of muscles working.'

Clowns, robots and penguins will each be guided into practising and repeating a two- or three-part pattern of movement associated with these well-known images. The whole dance itself follows a repeating pattern as each of the groups is started and stopped in turn.

Lesson Plan – 25 minutes

Theme:
Winter

WARM-UP ACTIVITIES - 4 minutes

1 All stand well spaced, where you can see me. I will sing the words slowly so that you can join in, saying the words as well as doing the actions which must be big and lively.

This is the way we try to keep warm,
try to keep warm, try to keep warm, (running on the spot with high knee raising and big arm swinging)
this is the way we try to keep warm,
on a cold and frosty morning.

This is the way we bend and stretch,
bend and stretch, bend and stretch, (feet wide, bend and stretch knees and arms high)
this is the way we bend and stretch,
on a cold and frosty morning.

MOVEMENT SKILLS TRAINING - 13 minutes

1 Show me gentle swirling waters of a stream as it trickles, curving round a bend or bubbling over stones. Let your whole body be part of the curving and the turning.

2 Slowly the frost comes down. The stream slows, freezes and stops. Show me your different, jagged shapes becoming hard and spiky.

3 Here comes the sun, and the ice softens, loses its hard, jagged shape and starts, slowly at first, to flow again.

4 Near the stream is a house with water drip, drip dripping down from the snow on the roof. With your fingers and arms, show me what this long trickling, dripping water looks like. (Fingers wriggle quickly. Arms reach up and down. Knees bend and stretch.)

5 The frost comes and the dripping water slowly turns into a long, hard, stiff, jagged icicle. Show me! Drip again . . . . freeze! Make your long, thin, frozen, still shapes. Feel hard and stiff.

6 Here comes the sun. The icicles start to smooth out, lose their sharpness and drip, drip, drip again in that long, wriggly line.

DANCE - Frosty Winter - 8 minutes

1 Half of the class will move like the little stream, all round the room. The other half stay in their places, to move like the water dripping down from the roof. Show me your starting shape.

2 Streams, flow slowly, curving, trickling, twisting, with your whole body working as you flow along.

3 Roof top trickles, start to drip, drip, drip, in a long, thin line as you fall to the ground, plop, plop, plop.

4 The frost comes and makes the drips from the house turn into icicles, long, thin, hard, jagged shapes.

5 The stream starts to slow down, freeze and become solid. Hold your stiff, jagged shapes which will be wider and flatter than the long, thin icicles.

6 Everyone, feel stiff and firm. If I push you, I should not be able to make you move.

7 Here comes the sun and we all start, very slowly at first, to melt, trickle, move along and then flow normally again,

8 The stream will demonstrate its movements first, then we will look at the melting snow.

9 Observe; comment; change over actions; practise; perform; observe.

LESSON NOTES AND NC GUIDANCE

Pupils should be involved in performing and improving performance.

Desirable features of a successful performance include wholehearted and vigorous activity, sharing space sensibly and unselfishly, with a concern for one's own and others' safety; neatly linking actions together with control; and showing skilfulness, variety and contrast.

Throughout this lesson, larger than life body movements are being used to express aspects of Winter. In the shared choice teaching method used, the teacher suggests the nature of the activity and the pupils decide the exact actions.

'Can you make your whole body bubble, curve and turn like the stream?' 'Show me what the long dripping, trickling, melting snow looks like.' The dancer is using actions, shapes, rhythms and patterns to give a performance expressing 'Frosty Winter'.

Each group's demonstration of their half of the dance will help the other half with planning ideas when they change over. We remember what we see.

Lesson Plan – 25 minutes

Theme:
Heavy and light, strong and gentle, and the amount of tension used in the muscles.

WARM-UP ACTIVITIES - 4 minutes

1 Stand with your feet wide apart, giving you a strong grip to the floor. Bend your knees and arms and show me your strongest push by both hands up to the ceiling. Hold your wide, strong stretch!

2 Now feel as if you have no muscles in your arms, body or legs, and flop down – go! Stay hanging down, all floppy and loose.

3 Now firm up again and feel all those strong muscles lifting, twisting, pushing you up to the ceiling. Hold it firmly!

4 Suddenly relax, let go and – flop! (Repeat several times.)

MOVEMENT SKILLS TRAINING - 12 minutes

1 Feel strong in your legs and let me hear you running, beating the floor as firmly and quickly as you can, on your own spot. Go!

2 Pretend you are making huge splashes in a puddle. Splash, splash, splash, splash, heavy feet, pushing firmly.

3 Now pretend you are gently walking through a pool of water, trying not to make any splashes. Tip toe, tip toe, softly, softly.

4 Tip toe so softly that your magic feet might even tip toe on top of the water. Gently, gently.

5 There's a big, heavy weight in front of you that needs to be moved. It's blocking your way. Bend your knees and push it with your arms, shoulders, back and legs. Heave! Feel your strong muscles.

6 In front of you, now, is a huge balloon. Push it lightly away and walk along behind it, push, push, pushing it so gently that it doesn't fly away from you. Fingertips, fingertips, easy flicking.

7 Show me how your huge balloon might float along if it were being gently pushed by you. It will be slow, silent, rising and falling, sometimes turning, sometimes hanging, still, in the air.

DANCE - Light and Heavy Opposites - 9 minutes

1 Find a partner and plan an 'Opposites' dance. For example, one of you might start by pushing a heavy weight, your partner, slowly and with difficulty straight along the floor. The person being pushed will be heavy, firm, near to the floor. Then you change over. The one being pushed becomes the pusher and the partner becomes a big, light, easy to move balloon. Pushing is easy and the travelling is light and floating. You choose. Try my idea or one of your own.

2 Big splashes in the puddle, side by side, followed by tip toeing on water might be another idea, with more travelling to do.

3 Punch, punch, punch, punch, heavy, strong movements against one partner (no contact!) sends that partner slowly stumbling back, step by step. In the opposite direction, the partner, now moving forwards, can gently flick a speck of dust in the air backwards with little, light bouncy steps.

4 Sit down, please. I have given you some ideas and many of you have planned your own ideas. We'll look at half of the class at a time, performing their favourite and best 'Opposites' dance. Look for and tell me about couples who change well from heavy to light, strong to gentle, with good, clear actions.

LESSON NOTES AND NC GUIDANCE

Pupils should be taught to try hard to improve and consolidate performances, alone, with a partner, and in a group.

The teacher in Physical Education is fortunate that the lessons are so visual, allowing the whole class to be seen performing. Assessment of pupils' achievement and progress is of an overall performance, not the isolated parts that combine to make it. The finished piece of dance is the 'performance' referred to in the above requirements.

If 'Dancing is about using your imagination', the teacher begins by explaining the theme to the class, giving them good images to stir their imaginations. The use of images in the middle part of the lesson helps the class to work more quickly and with understanding. Partners will then plan their own images and 'pictures in their head' as they respond to the challenge to plan and perform an 'Opposites' dance as the outcome of the topic's development.

Imagery inspires the actions, making them specific and clear. A rhythmic pattern of joined up movements helps partners repeat, improve and remember their dance. Encouraging, helpful observations from both teacher and class leads to further progress and feelings of pleasure and enhanced confidence.

Lesson Plan – 25 minutes

Theme:
Simple, traditional dance steps and figures.

WARM-UP ACTIVITIES - 5 minutes

1 Skip by yourself to this lively country dance music. Try to do the skipping step as I call out 'Skip, skip, skip, skip' so that we are all keeping with the music. Skip, skip, skip, skip; 5, 6, 7, 8.

2 This time, see if you have a different foot forwards each time I call out 'Skip!' Skip, skip, skip, skip, change feet, change feet; one foot forwards, the other foot; one foot forwards, the other foot.

3 Keep skipping in time to the music, but listen for my drum beats. Two beats mean join hands and dance with a partner. One beat means separate and dance by yourself.

TEACH STEPS AND FIGURES OF THE LESSON'S FOLK DANCE - 14 minutes

1 Stand next to a partner in our big circle, where you can all see me. Put your hands by your sides. I will come round and give you each a number – one or two.

2 Hands up the ones. Hands up the twos. Good. All correct.

3 Number ones, skip into the circle for four counts and clap your hands. Dance back out for four counts.

4 Number twos, do the same. Don't hurry. Take all four steps and clap hands on '4'. Use all four counts to come out again.

5 Face your partner. Give your partner one hand. Turn each other right round for four counts one way, then back with the other hand in the opposite direction for four counts.

6 Stand side by side, facing the way I am showing you (anti-clockwise). Give both hands to your partner and promenade round in our big circle for eight counts.

DANCE - Circle Folk Dance - 6 minutes

Music   Any lively, 32-bar English or Scottish dance tune.

Formation   A big circle, next to a partner, numbered one or two.

Bars 1–8   Ones dance to the centre, clapping hands on '4', and dance out again, back to places.

Bars 9–16   Twos dance into the centre, clapping hands on '4', and dance out again, back to places.

Bars 17–24   Partners face each other and turn, giving one arm for four, and turn back to places, giving other arm.

Bars 25–32   Partners all face anti-clockwise, and give both hands to each other to promenade round in the circle for eight counts.

Repeat.

LESSON NOTES AND NC GUIDANCE

Pupils should be taught to perform movements or patterns, including some from existing dance traditions and from different times and cultures.

The folk dance lesson often starts with pupils standing, clapping hands in time with the rhythmic beat of the music, and counting out the '1, 2, 3, 4, 5, 6, 7, 8'-beat phrases of the music. Skipping, and trying to make each step on to your front foot hit the beat of the music, then follows. Skipping is a '1, 2, 3' action, so a different foot should lead into each skip change of step, as we go. 'Right, 2, 3; left, 2, 3; right, 2, 3; left, 2, 3; skip, 2, 3; skip, 2, 3.'

With young beginners in folk dance, a circle formation is the easiest to use. All can see and follow the teacher as he or she walks slowly through the figures of the typical four parts of the dance. We walk it through, then skip it through, then try it with the music, helped all the way by the teacher's rhythmic accompaniment of the steps as a reminder and to ensure that each of the four parts of the dance receives its full eight counts. Four parts, each of eight bars of the music, is a typical pattern for a folk dance, whether it is teacher-created, as this one is, or a traditional dance of long standing.

Lesson Plan – 25 minutes

Theme:
Watching a moving object suggest ways of moving.

WARM-UP ACTIVITIES - 5 minutes

1 Balance on tip toes, arms and legs straight, one foot in front of the other.

2 Stride out smartly, still with arms and legs straight, hurrying forwards, but looking up.

3 Push up high off one foot, reaching up with the opposite hand. Who can jump up the highest? Land with a nice, squashy landing on both feet and return to your starting, tip toes position.

4 Ready. Balance on tip toes; stride out firmly, with straight arms and legs; spring up from one foot and do your highest-ever jump.

MOVEMENT SKILLS TRAINING - 15 minutes

1 Listen to the words, and watch the bubbles being blown by several girls and boys. 'Floating calmly, gliding smoothly, soaring, sinking. Pop! All gone!'

2 Let's all say the words together as we watch other children make their bubbles fly. (Repeat words, very slowly, to accompany the several actions through to the end.)

3 We'll take each part separately and make neat actions as we think about how bubbles move. 'Floating calmly', silently on tip toes, arms lifting you up, body turning, spinning, feeling no weight. Look at the way some bubbles are going up and down.

4 'Gliding smoothly', a little quicker, more streamlined in space. Straighten out and do big curves to turn. How will you hold your arms to help your smooth gliding action?

5 In 'soaring' we start low and gradually increase speed to a higher level. Look up as you travel, reaching high and keeping your shape. Be streamlined and smooth. Down, down, up, up, up.

6 'Sinking' starts from a high position, gradually falling with no jerkiness, smoothly to the floor.

7 'Pop! All gone!' is the one quick movement. It could be a tiny jump; or arms and legs suddenly opening and closing quickly; or a drop down to a curled or stretched position on the floor.

DANCE - Bubbles - 5 minutes

1 Show me your still, lifted starting shape. I will say each set of words as your signal to show me how your bubble is moving. 'Floating calmly' – lifting, turning, gently along, up and down.

2 'Gliding smoothly' – a more streamlined, straighter pathway, arms in the glide, curving to turn.

3 'Soaring' – drop down low and travel straight, rising right up on to tip toes. A clear, streamlined body shape.

4 'Sinking' – from your highest balance, travel slowly along, dropping gradually. Smooth all the way.

5 'Pop! All gone!' – a quick move and be still. (Repeat. Improve the quality – how slow; how light; how gentle; how sudden? Perform.)

LESSON NOTES AND NC GUIDANCE

Pupils should be taught to use good posture and clear body shapes as they demonstrate good control, co-ordination, balance, poise, turning and stillness.

It has been said that 'In dance we move more fully than in everyday life', and in certain lessons the dancer is challenged to perform in a larger than life, semi-exaggerated manner, bringing every part of the body into the action.

Use of imagery once again gives the dancer a well-known, moving object to relate to. The dancer is not 'being' a bubble. He or she is moving, expressing the movement characteristics of the bubble, with its floating, hovering, lighter than air; its gentle, smooth, curving, gliding; its streamlined soaring; and its soft, turning, falling to its sudden 'Pop! All gone!'

This slow dance is an excellent contrast to the usual high speed movement of young pupils. Representing the movement qualities of the slow, light, gentle object moving in space demands a well-controlled, balanced and poised use of the whole body.

Lesson Plan – 25 minutes

Theme:
Space, directions and levels.

WARM-UP ACTIVITIES - 5 minutes

1 Stand with your feet apart for balance, letting your fingers walk up to the space high above your head. Really stretch up, right up on to tip toes.

2 Lower your straight arms down, feeling the space at your sides.

3 How far can you reach out in front of you with one hand? Bend your knees to help your balance. Now twist with the other hand to touch the space behind you.

4 Touch hips; touch knees; touch ankles; touch toes; touch the floor. Coming back up, touch the floor again; toes; ankles; knees; and hips.

5 Can you remember your own space? I want you to travel to visit a side, an end, a corner, the middle, and then come back to your own space. Make your travelling so neat, quiet and interesting that I want to look at it. (Look out for walking, skipping, hopping, bouncing, running, jumping, galloping, gliding, floating.)

MOVEMENT SKILLS TRAINING - 13 minutes

1 Watch these six travellers whose neat actions made me want to look at them. Thomas is tip toeing quickly. Amy is bouncing with a twist. Joe is running and jumping. Rosie is leaping along with long arms and legs swinging. Adam is hopping, three times on each foot. Meera is skipping with high knees and arms.

2 Try out some of those excellent actions to travel round. When I beat the tambourine and say 'Change!' can you be very clever and change to a new action, in a different direction, forwards, or sideways, or very carefully going backwards? Try to find out which actions are good for going sideways and backwards – and use your eyes to look for spaces. Go!

3 Let's travel with different body parts going first and leading us. Nose . . . . one elbow . . . . back . . . . toes . . . . seat . . . . chest . . . . side of one leg . . . . knees. Did you see how often you changed directions?

DANCE - Space Dance - 7 minutes

1 Choose your own starting space, well away from all the others. First with your hands by themselves, then with your feet by themselves, show me how you can reach to different levels to touch the spaces above, to the sides and behind you. A nice pattern would be 'Hands reach high; to the sides; behind; down low. One foot reaches forwards and to the side, the other reaches back and kicks up high.'

2 Travel to visit a side, end, corner and the middle of the room. Try to use a variety of neat actions that take you in different directions with different body parts leading.

3 Find a partner and both stand, sharing the same space. To give our 'Space Dance' more variety we will have the number one partners staying in their spaces to start, while number twos travel away from and back to the shared space, after carefully dancing around all those working in their spaces. Partners then change places and actions.

4 Have another practice, then we will look at each half of the class in turn. Work hard to reach many spaces on the spot. Show me beautiful travelling actions in many directions.

5 Perform; comment; repeat; improve; perform again.

LESSON NOTES AND NC GUIDANCE

Pupils should be involved in the continuous process of planning, performing and evaluating, and the greatest emphasis should be placed on the actual performance.

At the start of the lesson the teacher will put the class 'in the picture' regarding the lesson's theme. Such advance information is essential and fair, particularly if some form of assessment is being made of the created dance climax of the lesson.

The lesson's beginning, middle and end should all relate to, and lead up to, the creation of a dance. Only in this way can pupils know where they are; show, perform and feel; and understand and repeat.

Various ways to move to touch all of one's own personal space are identified, practised, commented on, and improved.

Various ways to travel to a new space are encouraged by the teacher's commentary, praising good actions as they happen, and through demonstrations of neat, quiet, lively actions.

The challenge for partners to 'Plan a "Space Dance", with one dancing on the spot and the other travelling to a space and back again, then both changing over their actions' is easy to respond to, because the lesson has led up to the creation of such a dance.

Lesson Plan – 25 minutes

Theme:
Spring and growth.

WARM-UP ACTIVITIES - 6 minutes

1 Stand with your feet wide apart, and your upper body and arms hanging down. Slowly stretch up with arms reaching high and wide above your head. Drop arms back to your bent forwards position.

2 Feel your body growing, then collapsing. Stretch high and wide, 2, 3. Arms and body drop, 2, 3. Keep practising.

3 Can you try the same actions from a tiny, curled up, kneeling position? Now stretch back, shoulders and arms out wide. Can you feel your strong, firm stretch right through to your fingertips? Bend your arms, shoulders, and back to your curled up, tiny finish.

4 Stand up and do three walking steps then a high jump, pushing straight up with both arms swinging high above your head. Step, step, step and spring! Step, step, step, spring high! Feel yourself growing very tall as you jump high in the air.

MOVEMENT SKILLS TRAINING - 7 minutes

1 Kneel down and curl to your smallest shape. Show me how you can start to grow, very slowly. Are you starting with your back, head, shoulders, elbows or arms? Show me clearly how you are rising to a full, wide stretch position.

2 Gently, return to your curled up starting position and practise growing, very slowly, once again.

3 Are you rising straight up, or with a little twist from side to side? Maybe one shoulder, elbow or hand leads, then the other in an interesting, twisting way to rise and grow.

DANCE - Spring Dance · 12 minutes

1 Find a partner and both kneel down near each other for the first part of our 'Spring Dance' – the flower seed growing. Curl up small, close to the floor.

2 Slowly, start to grow and show me which parts of you are leading as you rise slowly to your full, wide flower shape. You might even twist your full flower shape to look at the sun. (Teacher, moving slowly, can represent the sun as a focus.)

3 Let's have a look at our partner's way of rising, growing and stretching out towards the sunshine. Decide who is going first.

4 Now the other partner. Can you surprise your partner and me by making a sudden stretch into your final stretch shape? Begin.

5 Well done, everyone. I saw lots of beautiful growing actions and flower shapes, Can the

first partner stand now for the second part of our dance – mother bird and baby bird. Mother bird flies round the nest, looking for food for the kneeling baby bird in the nest, reaching and stretching up to receive the food brought by the mother, who then flies off again. Practise your flying, collecting food, and your reaching up and receiving the food.

6 Mother bird now thinks that the baby is old enough to rise up and fly away from the nest. Mother signals 'Come on, follow me', and the baby slowly rises, tries out its wings, and follows the mother, occasionally stumbling, falling and getting up again.

7 That was really good, mothers and babies. Let's practise the whole dance from the beginning, then look at lots of couples.

LESSON NOTES AND NC GUIDANCE

Pupils should be able to show that they can improve performance, through practice, alone and with a partner.

Prior to an improved performance, there must be:

a a clear understanding of the specific nature of the lesson's theme. Vague descriptions such as 'We are exploring stretching and curling' or 'We are making shapes' are abstract and difficult to understand. They do not conjure up an easily visualised, clearly understood image. 'Our lesson is about the way that plants and birds start to grow in spring' will capture pupils' interest and tell them where the lesson is going.

b opportunities to be taught, experience, practise, repeat and be questioned about what we mean by growing actions, generally, from a curled up starting shape.

c discussion and practice of the more specific actions of a seed slowly growing and rising to a

full flower shape, or a baby bird rising slowly, trying out its wings, and making its first stumbling attempts at flying.

d a definite, clearly understood structure to the eventual dance, decided by the teacher. All vagueness is removed by the clear form of the dance: partners, near each other, both perform the seed growing at the start; one partner then stands to represent the mother bird looking for, then offering food to the baby bird in the nest; the mother bird signals to the baby to try to rise up and fly away from the nest; the baby is unsteady to start with, but eventually manages the action.

Lesson Plan – 25 minutes

Theme:
Feelings.

WARM-UP ACTIVITIES - 5 minutes

1 Help me, please, by saying the words and doing the actions, as we do our lively walking or skipping round together.

If you're happy and you know it, clap your hands,
If you're happy and you know it, clap your hands,
If you're happy and you know it, and you really want to show it,
If you're happy and you know it, clap your hands.

If you're happy and you know it, smile and wave,
. . . . twist and shake . . . . jump for joy . . . .

MOVEMENT SKILLS TRAINING - 13 minutes

1 Without travelling from where you are now, show me a happy face. Show me a whole body shape that tells me you are happy.

2 Show me an angry face . . . . angry hands . . . . angry whole body.

3 Well done. You are using your body and parts of your body to show me feelings. Now show me a proud body with its proud back, head, arms – very pleased with yourself.

4 Now you are frightened. Show it in your face and your whole body, hiding, shrinking away from something unpleasant.

5 Well done. All those feelings were shown on the spot. Can you try to use body activities to show me your feelings now? How about dancing around, happily waving your arms?

6 Still travelling, show me your angry feet stamping the floor and your angry hands punching the air.

7 Clever girls and boys, let me see your swaggering, very proud walking, like someone very important. Look at me! I'm the best!

8 Fear now, as you rush away, stop to look back, hide away from that terrible something behind you, following you. You might even have to crouch down low, as you hide from it.

DANCE - Feelings - 7 minutes

1 Find a partner and decide which of the feelings you want to use for our partners dance. Happy? Angry? Proud? Frightened?

2 Practise on the spot by yourself. Try to make a little pattern that you can remember and repeat, as you show me your own ways of moving to show your feelings. If I watch you, will I see a repeating pattern? (Encourage three or four parts to the short sequence on the spot, e.g. angry stamping, punching, jumping.)

3 Our dance will end with both of you dancing together. Decide what actions you will use. Will you skip and clap happily; stamp and punch angrily; swagger and step high proudly; or creep and hide, very frightened? Please decide and practise.

4 Before we practise the whole dance through, decide on your final shape and position that really shows me how you feel.

5 Show me your starting shape and position. My signals will be a drum beat for number one to start; a drum beat for number two to start; then a drum beat for your final part, together. Ready . . . .

6 Once more through, then we will share some of these brilliant ideas for showing feelings through our movements.

LESSON NOTES AND NC GUIDANCE

Pupils should be taught to explore moods and feelings and express and communicate ideas.

Expressing feelings through dance movement, rather than through speech or facial (acting) contortions, is not easy. The lesson's pattern and structure is designed to lead the class, bit by bit, through to the creation of the dance climax. After the easy 'Follow the teacher' opening song, expressing happiness through actions, the middle part of the lesson, with a lot of direct teaching, challenges the class to indulge wholeheartedly in big body movements to express happiness, anger, pride and fear, both in one's own space and while travelling.

Good examples will have been shared with the class who now understand that it is important to plan a movement expression. The teacher will have helped with examples from his or her repertoire.

The dance climax challenge is specific and therefore easily understood. The request to 'make a little pattern that you can remember and repeat' is in line with the joined up actions they have always been taught to use in their dance lessons.

The eventual dance will be unique with each one of the pair doing their own different dance, then combining to respond to each other in a third dance. 'Sharing some of these brilliant ideas for showing feelings through our movements' will therefore be an essential part of the lesson structure.

Lesson Plan – 25 minutes

Theme:
Vocal sounds as movement accompaniment and inspiration.

WARM-UP ACTIVITIES - 5 minutes

1 Listen to the rhythm of the lively music as you walk, skip, run, bounce or run and jump. When I sound the tambourine twice, find a partner and dance together. You can be joined or separate. Go!

2 When the tambourine sounds once, separate and dance by yourself.

3 When the tambourine sounds twice, find a partner, different to the one you had last time, and dance together.

MOVEMENT SKILLS TRAINING - 10 minutes

1 I am going to sing out some of the actions we have done in our Dance lessons. Listen very carefully and see if you can keep going with my words. Some of the words might be stretched out and others might be shortened. Are you ready?

2 W-a-l-k; be still; f-l-o-p; stretch; sk-i-i-p; stamp; t-u-r-n; clap; c-u-r-l; balance. Well done. You kept with me splendidly.

3 We can also move to other words that aren't movement words. Try moving to 'Tick tock' just where you are. Say it and do it for me. Tick tock, small move, tick tock, light and quick.

4 Show me how you can travel to a wind blowing sound – whoosh!

5 Can you be brilliant and invent a sound or two sounds I have never heard before, and show me how you can move to them? Join the sounds and the movements exactly together.

6 Make your movements and your shapes very neat and let me hear your invented sounds loud and clear.

DANCE - Voice Sounds - 10 minutes

1 You have been making your own sounds to accompany your varied movements. Can you think of anything you might be doing, or any place where you might be going during the holidays, that might help us to make our last dance together for this school year? Suggest some of the action words that might be used to accompany a short dance if we stretch out or shorten parts of the word. Swimming . . . . paddling . . . . flying . . . . playing . . . . driving . . . . shopping . . . . painting.

2 Can anyone tell me a place where you might be going that is an interesting word to dance to? Florida . . . . Glasgow . . . . Majorca . . . . Bournemouth . . . . Vancouver . . . . Scotland.

3 Decide your action word or a place, and then practise your short dance, saying the word and trying to include some stillness, travelling, a jump, and maybe a turn or a rise and fall.

4 Take a deep breath before you start so that you can make one or more parts of the word s-t-r-e-e-t-ch out and be interesting to listen to and watch.

5 Finish your little dance, beautifully still and with a shape that makes me want to look at you.

6 Well done everyone. I see lots of good action and I hear lots of interesting voice sounds. Let's have each half of the class in turn looking at and commenting on the other half.

7 When you are watching, look out for and tell me about good actions, good shapes and excellent use of the voice that made the word good for movement.

LESSON NOTES AND NC GUIDANCE

Pupils should be able to show that they can:

a *plan and perform simple skills safely.*

b *show control in linking actions together.*

In the lively warm-up travelling start to the lesson, there will be much revision of the many and varied travelling actions, and requests from the teacher for neat, quiet controlled footwork often illustrated by a quick demonstration. There will also be the request for safe travelling, always looking for 'good spaces, visiting all parts of the room – the sides, ends, corners as well as the middle, and never following anyone.'

In addition to practising safely and well, the skills of travelling are practised rhythmically to the accompanying music.

The teacher's voice is the rhythmic accompaniment to the idea of stretching and shortening well-known actions in the middle part of the lesson. Pupils are then challenged to invent a sound and plan how to move to it, showing clear shapes and neat movement.

In the created dance climax of the lesson, pupils start off with an action or place word, and then have to plan a pattern of varied speed actions, trying to include 'some stillness, travelling, a jump and maybe a turn or a rise and fall.' This is a double challenge, namely to link several actions smoothly and to include interesting and possibly exciting changes of speed to make the sequence more spectacular.

Lesson Plan – 25 minutes

Theme:
Awareness of basic actions and contrasts of shape.

WARM-UP ACTIVITIES - 5 minutes

1 Let's all join hands in a nice, big, round circle to sing and move together.

Let's join hands in one big ring,	(arms swing forwards and back)
Let's join hands and let us sing,	(add knees bend and stretch)
Let's join hands both high and low,	(arms swing high at same time as knees stretch)
Let's drop hands and wave 'Hello!'	

Let's all bounce in one big ring,	(quiet, springy, upward jumps)
Let's all bounce and bounce and sing,	
Let's keep bouncing, nice and slow,	
Now shake hands and say 'Hello!'	

MOVEMENT SKILLS TRAINING - 15 minutes

1 Well done, singers and dancers. That was a lively, friendly way to start. Stand in your own good space, now, and show me some of the actions that we can do on the spot to this lively, jazzy music.

2 I can see walking; marching; bouncing; skipping; stamping; running; balancing by rising and lowering on tip toes. Practise, thinking of actions that use your feet and legs.

3 Be very clever now and add a body movement to whatever you are doing with your feet and legs. For example – stepping and clapping; bouncing and turning; stamping and gesturing. Remember, we are working on the spot – not travelling!

4 Let's look at some very good examples now.

5 Using the same lively music, let me see you travelling to visit all parts of the room. All together . . . . best walking . . . . best skipping . . . . best bouncing. . . . best hopping. . . .

6 As you travel this time, show me different body shapes to make it more interesting. Ready. . . . Go!. . . . walking (tall, arms stretched upwards or feet and arms wide) . . . . skipping (curled with arms in to sides or high, stretched leading arm and leg). . . . bouncing (twisted with upper body facing behind or very straight body and arms at sides) . . . . hopping (curled, wide or stretched).

DANCE - The Snake - 10 minutes

1 Find a partner and stand, one behind the other, to make a little snake whose front actions will be copied by its back part. A snake's actions ripple down its body from head to tail.

2 Leaders, you are going to take your partner to different parts of the room, always looking for good spaces. Show your partner two or three actions and clear shapes to copy. Keep repeating those different actions so that you can remember them. Go!

3 Well done. Your snakes kept travelling beautifully and you are repeating your little pattern of two or three actions. Change places. The new leader can add an action on the spot before leading in to your two or three travelling actions. Begin.

4 Practice; performance; comments; improved practice.

LESSON NOTES AND NC GUIDANCE

Pupils should be taught to:

a *respond readily to instructions*

b *be physically active*

c *be mindful of others*

d *be aware of the safety risks of inappropriate clothing, footwear and jewellery.*

At the start of a school year the lesson's main emphases include:

a establishing a tradition of immediate and wholehearted responses to instructions. Good behaviour, expressed in listening quietly and then doing what was asked, is essential if all, including the teacher, are to enjoy action-filled, almost non-stop lessons.

b aiming to make lessons 'scenes of busy activity', with everyone working and no-one waiting. The instant-action starting song in the circle where all can see and be seen by the teacher; the lively travelling with teacher direction in the middle part of the lesson; and the simple, ongoing, partners travelling dance climax, all contribute to near non-stop action.

c working together sensibly and cooperatively, unselfishly sharing the floor space, and expressing pleasure and appreciation for demonstrations by others.

d all being safely and sensibly dressed.

Lesson Plan – 30 minutes

Theme:
Body parts awareness.

WARM-UP ACTIVITIES - 5 minutes

1 I will read this poem slowly. Listen carefully and show me how well you can do the actions.

Nod your head, bend your knees,
Grow as tall as Christmas trees.
On your knees, slowly fall,
Curl yourself into a ball.
Raise your head, jump up like so,
Wave your hand and say 'Hello!'

2 I will read the poem once again, and help me with the words if you remember them. Think about all the different ways our clever bodies can move.

MOVEMENT SKILLS TRAINING - 15 minutes

1 You danced to the poem beautifully – and remembered lots of the words. Let's see if we can practise, then remember, sets of three actions. Use your feet first. They are very important parts in movement.

2 Bounce your heels a little way off the floor, toes touching the floor. Bounce heels, bounce heels, 3, 4; bounce low, bounce low, 3, 4; springy, springy, springy, stop! Now step smartly with a lift of your front leg. Step, step, 3 and 4; stepping smartly, 3 and 4.

3 Stay where you are and stamp firmly. Stamp, stamp, 3 and 4; on the spot, 3, 4; bump, bump, bump for 4; stamp, stamp, 3 and stop!

4 Perform all three parts again, four counts to each. Ready? Bounce, bounce, heels bounce; step forwards, 3, 4; stamp, stamp, start again. Bounce, 2, 3, 4; step, 2, 3, 4; stamp, 2, 3 and stop! Good. We all kept together.

5 Hands and arms now, clapping first. Clap, 2, 3, again. Clap, 2, 3, 4. Clap, 2, 3, 4. Now let arms swing forwards and back, just like when we walk. Swings, swings, lively swings; 1, 2, 3, 4. Again, and let your shoulders twist to make the swings bigger. Swing, swing, big swings; reach, reach, 3 and 4.

6 Shake hands – as if you were shaking them to dry them. Shake, shake, shake, shake; 1, 2, 3, 4; dry them, 2, 3, 4; quick-shake, 2, 3, stop!

DANCE - Clever Feet and Hands - 10 minutes

1 Listen to the rhythm of the music. 1, 2, 3, 4; 1, 2, 3, 4. Keep that speed as you bounce, step, stamp for four counts. Think about and 'feel' your feet. Go! Bounce, bounce, 3, 4; step 2, 3, 4; stamp on the spot, 3, 4; bounce, 2, 3, 4; step, 2, 3, 4; stamp, 2, 3 and stop!

2 That was excellent. Three very different leg actions. Now hands only. Clap, 2, 3, 4; swing, 2, 3, 4; shake, 2, 3, 4; clap, 2, 3, 4; swing, 2, 3, 4; shake, 2, 3 and stop! Good, everyone.

3 Now, can you be very clever and join together the three leg and the three hand actions? With the music, begin. Bounce-clap, bounce-clap, bounce-clap, 4; step-swing, step-swing, step-swing, 4; stamp-shake, stamp-shake, stamp-shake, 4. (Repeat for practice.)

4 Well done. This is very difficult and you managed it splendidly. We could call our dance 'Clever Hands and Feet and Clever Girls and Boys!' Let's have half the class looking at and enjoying the other half. Then we can talk about the things we particularly liked.

LESSON NOTES AND NC GUIDANCE

Pupils should be able to show that they can show control in linking actions together in ways that suit the activities.

Being able to plan and perform a series of joined up actions neatly and with control is the main requirement within the National Curriculum. If a pupil can remember and repeat such a sequence, he or she is proving the ability:

a to plan, showing an understanding of what was asked for;

b to perform more than one skill at a time by linking actions thoughtfully; and

c to be able to practise and improve his or her performance.

The pattern of doing joined up actions runs right through the lesson, as it should do right through infant school. There are eight simple actions in the warm-up, all stimulated and given a rhythm by the spoken poem.

Three sets of joined up actions on the spot – bouncing, stepping and stamping – have a repeating rhythm, medium-speed music accompaniment in the middle of the lesson, expanded in the dance climax by adding hand and arm claps, and swings and shakes. Success at this requires the total attention and wholehearted effort being sought in the previous lesson.

Lesson Plan – 30 minutes

Theme:
Fireworks.

WARM-UP ACTIVITIES - 5 minutes

1 In our last lesson we made a 'Clever Feet and Hands' dance. Let's start by doing some movements that use most parts of our body. Swing arms forwards and back, then forwards and high above your head. Bend knees and swing arms down to let your hands brush the floor as they swing back. Arms swing forwards and up above head with knees and body stretching. Again. Swing forwards, back, and forwards and up; bend down, swing arms back and forwards, and high up again. Keep practising your swinging, bending and stretching.

MOVEMENT SKILLS TRAINING - 15 minutes

1 What words describe a rocket's action? Whoosh? Zoom? Bang?

2 What do these actions look like? Fast, straight, streamlined?

3 Before the rocket takes off we need to light the paper fuse. It splutters and sizzles, then the long thin rocket shoots off, soaring from low to high.

4 Everyone, ready for your low, thin, streamlined start in your rocket shape. Where will you zoom to? Ready? Go!

5 How will you explode? From small to big with a scatter of your whole body? Get ready to explode, scatter and fall down. Go!

6 Let's practise again as you splutter and sizzle. . . . Zoom, Whoosh. . . . explode and scatter. . . . twinkle, fall, glide down.

7 What are the movements of a Catherine wheel? A slow spin at the start gradually speeds up and throws out sparks. Then it slows down gradually and dies. Try the Catherine wheel movements and use your arms for spinning to stop you becoming dizzy. Show me your slow start, your speeding up, your slowing and dying.

8 What actions do the little bangers make you think of? Shooting and jumping here and there, unexpectedly in an uneven way.

9 Let me see your pattern of unexpected, quick jumping and running actions. Surprise me. Go!

10 Let's try each of the fireworks again and show me the main thing about each one. Ready, rockets? Go! Catherine wheels, go! Bangers, go! Well done. One more practice and you can accompany yourselves with your own sounds, Go!

DANCE - Fireworks - 10 minutes

1 That was excellent. You pleased me and surprised me. Now, you choose which one you want to be. Hands up. . . . rockets. . . . Catherine wheels . . . . bangers. Catherine wheels go first. Go!. . . . Now die away.

2 As the last Catherine wheel starts to slow . . . . jumping bangers start now.

3 When the last two bangers only are left. . . . Rockets sizzle, zoom, bang and scatter down like stars.

Alternative ending – one rocket can stray and land in the middle of the room among all the spent fireworks lying there. The whole group can represent the unlit bonfire and start to flicker like sparks and flames, with twitching elbows and shoulders, making little fires all over. Own vocal accompaniment can be used. 'Crackle . . . . shoot . . . . flicker . . . . 'Slowly the bonfire becomes quieter and dies.

LESSON NOTES AND NC GUIDANCE

Pupils should be taught to develop control, co-ordination, balance, poise and elevation in the basic actions of travelling, jumping, turning, gesturing and stillness.

From the 'Clever Feet and Hands' dance of the previous lesson, we move on to clever whole bodies, working expressively to represent varied firework actions.

Everyone practises the three different actions in the middle of the lesson, with much questioning by the teacher to inspire a thoughtful, planned, focused response. A repeating pattern of each action is asked for so that the performers are able to remember, repeat, improve and express the movement characteristics of each.

The dance climax, to which all the practising has led, does call for stillness while waiting one's turn; then exciting, whole body travelling and zooming, spinning and turning, shooting and jumping; and finally gestures, as they shoot, explode, whirl, leap about, then crackle and flicker.

Lesson Plan – 30 minutes

Theme:
Christmas and toys.

WARM-UP ACTIVITIES - 5 minutes

1 Find a partner for 'Follow My Leader'. The leader pretends the partner is just learning to move and has to be shown, very carefully, how to use the different parts of the body. Make your movements 'larger than life' and let's see if you can make a little pattern of three actions, exactly together.

2 Following partner, you lead now and show me your 'larger than life' ways to move feet, legs, arms, shoulders, or the whole body.

MOVEMENT SKILLS TRAINING - 15 minutes

1 Keep the same partner, well spaced out all over the room, facing each other. One of you will be the puppet maker with your hammer and chisel. The other will be the still, solid block of wood.

2 Puppet maker, chisel out the head shape. Show your puppet how a head can move up, down, side to side, and rotate. Puppet, copy.

3 Puppet maker, work on the shoulders and show how they can lift and lower, go forwards and back, and do circular motions.

4 Arms are shaped next with long, up and down chisel movements. The bending, stretching, swinging and circling are then copied.

5 The body shape and the big body movements of bending, stretching, twisting and turning are made and demonstrated.

6 Legs are the most important body part. The puppet maker has to crouch low to shape out the legs and feet. Big actions of bending to the front and sides and swinging are shown and copied on the spot.

7 Legs can do much more than swing, bend and step on the spot. They can take you to all parts of the room. Some puppet makers choose to do 'Follow My Leader' with their puppets. Others, with hands high above the puppet's head, suspend them from strings. Mirroring or dangling, the puppets are guided through the varied travelling actions. They walk, skip, run, hop, bounce, jump with full use of the neck, arms, shoulders and legs just created.

DANCE - Puppet Makers - 10 minutes

Music   Beethoven's 9th, Choral Symphony – *Ode to Joy* (2 mins 18 secs).

1   From the beginning with the still, solid lump of wood, the puppet makers hammer and chisel the shape of head, shoulders, arms, body, feet and legs. At each stage, they demonstrate and lead the growing puppet through the body movements of each. Puppet makers travel with their own puppets as they visit all parts of the room. Movements are 'larger than life'.

2   All this hammering, chiselling and moving has been hard work. The puppets are hung up on a hook in the workshop and the puppet makers lie down for a well-earned rest and sleep on the floor.

3   The puppets have enjoyed their play-like travels so much that they jump down off their wall hooks and all dance round.

4   The puppet makers waken and are angry to see their puppets out of place. They chase after their own puppet who dodges away.

5   Puppets are caught and gripped firmly with one hand. The other hand points and gestures 'Naughty puppet! Behave yourself!'

LESSON NOTES AND NC GUIDANCE

Pupils should be taught to explore feelings and develop their response to music through Dance by using rhythmic responses. Pupils should be able to improve performance, through practice, alone and with a partner.

In this easy dance the pupils can almost be talked through the whole dance by the teacher, who guides them through the timings of each part. 'Chisel out the head shape, front, sides, back, top. Now show your puppet how its head can move. Puppets, watch and copy.' A repeating pattern at each stage will be helpful in remembering, repeating and improving the dance. 'Show your puppet how legs can swing forwards and back, forwards and back; step, step on the spot; swing to one side, swing to other side; swing forwards and back, forwards and back; step, step, on the spot; swing to one side, swing to other side.'

'Feelings' being expressed will include the weariness of the hard working puppet makers as they sag slowly to rest on the floor; the happiness of the puppets as they travel and try out all the enjoyable play-like movements possible in their clever bodies; the surprise and annoyance in the puppet makers when they waken and see the badly behaved puppets; and the excitement of the puppets at the games of chase.

Lesson Plan – 30 minutes

Theme:
Winter.

1 Let's sing and move to keep warm, pretending we are outside.

*This is the way we skip to keep warm,
skip to keep warm, skip to keep warm,
This is the way we skip to keep warm,
on a cold and frosty morning.*

*This is the way we big bend and stretch,
big bend and stretch, big bend and stretch,*   (bend knees to touch floor, high stretch)
*This is the way we big bend and stretch,
on a cold and frosty morning.*

(Repeat several times.)

1 If I asked you to do a 'Winter' drawing, what would you do?

2 'Snowflakes falling' is a good answer, thank you. Can you all move like a snowflake, slowly, gently, turning, hovering, falling?

3 'Wind bending the trees' is another good answer, thank you. Show me how the wind's strong, big, rushing movement is different to the snowflake's.

4 'Ice in a stream' is another excellent answer, thank you. Let me see you flowing like a stream, When I call 'Freeze!' show me how quickly you can stiffen into your rigid, jagged, icy shape.

DANCE - Winter - 10 minutes

WIND	SWOOSH	WHIRL	DROP
SNOWFLAKE	FLOAT	HOVER	SINK
STREAM	RUSH	FREEZE	MELT

1 Find a partner. One of you will collect a card and the other will pick up a piece of percussion.

2 Find a good floor space and look at the three action words on your card. Please do not look at other couples' cards. Three different cards are being used for our 'Winter dance'. Each card also tells you what is doing the three actions.

3 Dancing partner, perform your three actions carefully for your partner to watch and then make helpful comments. Start when ready – without any percussion sounds at this stage.

4 Well done. Dancers, sit down and be given some friendly, helpful advice to improve your performance. Were the actions clear? Were the body shapes full and clear? Was the speed right?

5 The same dancer again, please. Partner with percussion, you may quietly accompany your partner, starting and stopping to make the three actions separate. Begin when ready, please.

6 Well done, everyone. The improvements were obvious. Now change places. No accompaniment this time. New dancer, begin when ready.

7 Dancers, sit down and listen to the helpful comments.

8 Same dancers practise again, using the good advice received.

LESSON NOTES AND NC GUIDANCE

Pupils should be involved in the continuous process of planning, performing and evaluating.

As well as asking him or herself 'Was my lesson filled with worthwhile, enjoyable and challenging activity, flowing almost non-stop from start to finish?', the teacher also needs to check 'Did I provide opportunities for thoughtful planning, challenging the pupils to think ahead to try to see an intended outcome? Did the lesson build up to an end of lesson performance of a created dance? Somewhere in the lesson did I provide opportunities for the class to see a demonstration and make friendly, helpful comments, evaluating what they had seen?'

In the shared choice teaching method used in the lesson, the teacher, with the help of action words on cards, decides the nature of the activity. The pupils then plan and decide the precise actions to be practised, repeated, improved and eventually presented.

The observing partner has to look carefully to identify the main features of the actions; reflect on their accuracy; and then sensitively suggest ways to bring about an improvement.

Lesson Plan – 30 minutes

Theme:
Traditional dance.

WARM-UP ACTIVITIES - 5 minutes

1 Partners, travel side by side, keeping in time with the music. One of you will decide your actions which each take eight bars of the music. Try to include two or three different actions. A change of direction on '8' looks very attractive.

2 Other partner, can you decide on actions to take your pair apart and then bring you together again? Separate for eight counts, then come together again for eight counts.

3 Partners, practise a four-part repeating pattern of travelling side by side; parting; closing; travelling together.

TEACH AND DANCE - Djatchko Kolo (Yugoslavian Folk Dance) - 20 minutes

Music   *Djatchko Kolo*, Society for International Folk Dancing (cassette and book 3).

Formation   An open circle with teacher at right hand open end.

This simple dance can be learned easily, with the teacher calling out and demonstrating each movement straight away with the music, and the class copying the teacher.

Figure 1	Bar 1	Beat 1	Step right foot to right.
		2	Close left foot to right foot.
		3	Step right foot to right.
		4	Swing left foot across right foot.
	Bar 2	Beats 1–4	Repeat **Bar 1** to the left, starting with left foot.
	Bars 3 and 4		Repeat all of above.
Figure 2	Bar 5	Beat 1	Step right foot to right.
		2	Swing left foot across right foot.
		3	Step left foot to left.
		4	Swing right foot across left foot.
	Bar 6	Beats 1–4	Repeat **Bar 5**.
Figure 3	Bars 7 and 8		Starting with right foot, seven little walking steps to right and point heel of left foot on the floor on '8'.
	Bars 9 and 10		Seven steps to left and point heel of right foot on the floor on '8'.

Keep repeating dance from beginning.

REVISE A FAVOURITE DANCE - 5 minutes

Ideally, this favourite dance, often chosen by the pupils, will contrast with the new dance of this lesson. It could be a revision of January's 'Winter' dance.

LESSON NOTES AND NC GUIDANCE

Pupils should be taught to perform movements or patterns, including some from existing dance traditions. Pupils should be able to show that they can show control in linking actions together.

A traditional Dance lesson has many attractions. The warm-up gives the lesson a lively, repeating, rhythmic start, always with the possibility of development into enjoyable partner activity. The four-part repeating pattern here gives opportunities for varied, creative activity which is a good balance to the formal steps and figures of the folk dance.

When the steps and patterns of the dance are easy, as here, pupils quickly gain the pleasure of learning, mastering, repeating and improving another dance for their expanding repertoire. The circle formation lends itself to all seeing and copying the teacher's lead from start to finish. The slow rhythm of the start of the dance, accompanied by the teacher's rhythmic accompaniment of the simple actions, provides an almost instantly learned dance. Improvement comes with repetitions of the dance, with a different emphasis each time. 'Keep the circle round; grip with hands higher than elbows; erect posture throughout; neat steps and swings.'

Lesson Plan – 30 minutes

Theme:
Creating simple characters in response to music.

WARM-UP ACTIVITIES - 5 minutes

1 Let's warm up with some actions that might describe types of people. Off we go, proud soldiers. March, march, swing your arms; left, right, left, right; lift your knees, lift your arms; 1, 2, 3, 4.

2 Well done, proud soldiers. Ready again? Dithery person, here and there; ooops, I don't know where I'm going; side to side, forwards and back; turn around, change my mind.

3 Well dithered! One more. Ready? Tired person, flop about; dangling arms and heavy head; dragging legs and sagging knees.

MOVEMENT SKILLS TRAINING - 15 minutes

1 Listen to the slow, swaggering-style rhythm of the music. Feel the 1, 2, 3, 4 repeating beat and imagine yourself as someone very important, stepping out confidently to it.

2 Let's try some proud, slow steps, just like a very self-confident policeman or policewoman might do. Go!

3 Well done. This time, pretend you are on your beat, patrolling the streets where you live. Turn corners; cross roads, looking right, left, right; and let your cocky head and shoulders say 'All's well. We don't have any baddies round here.'

4 That was excellent. You all look very cocky and proud. Now let's try some suspicious 'Baddie' movements as if you are sneaking along behind one of these very special coppers, silently keeping just out of sight. Use little runs, dodging behind bushes, letter boxes, in driveways or in doorways. Off you go!

5 Sometimes you will be close behind, copying the swaggering, cocky walking - and being a little bit cocky yourself. You can stop and start together; sometimes freeze while the copper looks around; even pretend to be simply reading a paper or looking at your watch. Let's pretend to be self-confident baddies. Go!

DANCE - Cops and Robbers - 10 minutes

Music The *Pink Panther* theme from *The Pink Panther* by Henry Mancini and his Orchestra (ND 80832).

1 Find a partner and decide who is copper and who is robber. Stand ready for our practice, our little game of chase. Let's see if the cops can do a repeating pattern of travelling so that the baddie can also repeat his or her pattern of secret following, weaving in and out, behind, side to side, close up copying and freezing still. Start with the music.

2 Well done, cocky cops and robbers. This time I will stop the music as a signal for the copper to turn suddenly and catch the baddie. Running away is not allowed, you baddies! The goodies will grab hold with one hand and hold their truncheons above their partner's head with the other hand, expressing 'Gotcha!' The poor loser will express 'It's a fair cop, officer'. Ready? Go! (for about one minute, then the music is suddenly stopped).

3 Hold your positions, please. Well done. Now relax and we'll look at each half of the class in turn to see the many brilliant ideas you have created. You can tell me which ones you like.

LESSON NOTES AND NC GUIDANCE

Pupils should be taught to express and communicate moods, ideas and feelings, and develop their response to music.

The 'feelings' referred to include the interesting contrast in the movement expressions of the confident, self-assured, slightly arrogant, swaggering policeman or policewoman, and the movement expressions of the equally cocky, self-assured, sometimes cheeky robber.

Pupils practise each of the two parts separately, sometimes adding individual, funny mannerisms to their big swaggering walkabout. A standing cop shines the toes of a boot on the back of the other trouser leg; sticks thumbs through the braces; twirls the baton; waves to the admiring public; occasionally looks bored at such a crime-free existence.

The pursuing robber, bursting with self-assurance, zig-zags along, out of sight and out of hearing of the copper, sometimes hiding, then rushing after him or her. Occasionally, the cockiness leads to a close shadowing, mimicking the copper's every move.

Both use larger than life, big body movements to express how pleased they are with themselves.

Lesson Plan – 30 minutes

Theme   Clowns.

Music   *TV Sport* from *Festival of Music* by Central Band of the R.A.F.

WARM-UP ACTIVITIES - 5 minutes

1 Let's try a warm-up which I call '8 : 4 : 2' and see if you can keep with me. Eight skips forwards . . . . go! Skip, 2, 3, 4, 5, 6, 7, stop!

2 Good. You all started and stopped with me. Now an easy four steps backwards . . . . go! Step, 2, 3 and stop!

3 We've gone forwards. We've gone backwards. What direction do you think we will go next?

Yes, sideways with two chasse steps. Do it slowly with me. Step to the side; close feet together; step to the side; close feet together. Now do it a little bit quicker. Side step, close; side step, close. Well done. Now let's try the whole of our '8 : 4: 2'. Skip forwards, 3, 4, 5, 6, 7, 8; step backwards, 3, 4; side step, close, side step, close. Excellent. Again . . . . go!

MOVEMENT SKILLS TRAINING - 15 minutes

1 In our last lesson we thought about and moved like several different sorts of people – soldiers, ditherers, tired people and cops and robbers. At Easter time, as at Christmas time, there are often circuses to visit. What do you call the funny performers in a circus? Yes, clowns.

2 Show me a funny clown walk, please. Can you turn your toes in a long way, swing your arms across your chest, and swing your shoulders up and down a long way?

3 You might try your funny walk going backwards and sideways as well as forwards. Four steps each way would be a nice pattern.

4 Try a funny walk on your heels, or your toes, or one of each. Add lots of funny, big, swinging arm, shoulder and head movements.

5 Clowns do lots of balancing on one foot and then suddenly stumble, nearly falling down as they do little running steps to save themselves. Show me your funny balance shapes and your wobbling, stumbling quick steps to balance still again.

6 Sometimes they do lose balance and sit down on to their bottom. Show me a balance on your bottom with legs stuck up in the air.

7 Now twist over on to your tummy and show me another funny balance, with arms and legs lifted and doing swimming actions.

1 Practise a pattern of funny walks, funny balances, staggers and runs to save yourself, and funny stumbles into a balance on bottom or chest, or one of each. Then jump up like 'Jack In The Box'.

2 Find a partner and pretend your partner needs cheering up. Find a good space for your little circus ring. One of you sit down as a spectator. The other one does his or her clown dance to include some funny walking, funny balancing, wobbling, staggering, and then a sit down and funny balance on your bottom or front, or both.

3 Well done. Have one more practice. You can use our 8 : 4: 2 pattern if you like – eight funny walks, four funny balances, wobbles and staggering about, and two balances, one on seat and one on chest.

4 Hands up all the spectators who laughed because you were amused? Can anyone tell me what you thought was good fun?

5 Change over now to a new clown and a new spectator. Start when you are ready. Clowns, dancers, give us a good laugh, please.

LESSON NOTES AND NC GUIDANCE

Pupils should be able to show that they can improve performance, through practice, alone and with a partner.

From performing the movement characteristics of hyper-confident cops and robbers, we move on to show the equally exaggerated, typical movements of a circus clown. The eventual performance by the clown has far greater potential for variety and interest, and for a repeating pattern of funny movements. The funny walking in all directions on all parts of the feet, the unstable, wobbly balancing on feet, the staggering run to regain balance, and the falling to balance on seat or back can all be fitted into a repeating, contrasting pattern that aids remembering and improvement.

Partners' observations and comments also aid the altering, adapting and extending that promote further planning and an improved performance.

Lesson Plan – 30 minutes

Theme:
Kittens.

WARM-UP ACTIVITIES - 5 minutes

1 Lots of baby animals are born in spring and they have to learn how to use their muscles to move.

2 With silent feet, weave in and out of one another, trying out the different ways your legs can travel. If you were a baby animal – lamb, puppy, kitten – you might try a little run and jump up.

3 Run a little way, jump high, then bend down towards the ground for a silent landing. Jump up and do a bendy, squashy landing. A baby animal doesn't want to hurt its bones and lands gently.

4 Often the baby animal springs up, twists in the air, and lands facing another way. Try a jump, twist and gentle landing.

MOVEMENT SKILLS TRAINING - 15 minutes

1 Let's think about how a kitten might try out its muscles. Lie curled up small on the carpet in your home. Can you roll over from one side of your body to the other side? Roll and roll; a curled-up roll; side to side; roll and roll. Well done, kittens.

2 Now sit up tall, and stretch out your body. Stretch up one paw, 1–4; pull it down, 5–8; stretch up the other paw, 1–4; pull it down, 5–8; stretch up both paws at the same time and this time try out your claws, 1–4; pull in your claws and paws, 5–8.

3 On hands and knees, try a whole body stretch and arch up high, 1–4; relax down again, 5–8; whole body arch high, 1–4; relax down again, 5–8.

4 Jump up from your carpet. Go out into your garden and try a run and a jump, landing gently. Not a sound! Do it two or three times and you can try a clever twist to land facing a different way.

5 Here's a high fence. Run and jump high to balance and walk along it, forwards then backwards, forwards then backwards.

6 Be clever and balance on one foot only on the fence, stretching out all parts of your body. Balance again, on the other foot.

7 It's time to go indoors. Jump down from your high fence and do a soft, squashy landing. Go back to your carpet starting places.

1 All lie curled up small on your nice soft carpet. Roll over from one side of your body to the other side. Roll and roll.

2 Sit up tall and straight and try out one paw as you stretch, 2, 3, 4; pull in, 2, 3, 4; other paw, stretch, 2, 3, 4; pull in, 2, 3, 4; both paws and claws, stretch, 2, 3, 4; pull in, 2, 3, 4.

3 On your hands and knees, try out your whole body arching up . . . . and down . . . . and arch high up . . . . and relax down.

4 Jump up and go out into the garden for a run and jump and a soft landing. Run, jump, land. Run, jump and twist and land. Now a really high jump up on to the fence.

5 Balance walk slowly forwards, backwards, forwards, backwards. Now on one foot only, stretch everything. On to the other foot and a big stretch of your whole body Really stretch.

6 Jump down very gently and walk back to your nice soft carpet.

REPETITION   PERFORMANCE   COMMENTS   IMPROVED PRACTICE

LESSON NOTES AND NC GUIDANCE

Pupils should be taught to adopt the best possible posture and use of the body as they perform imaginatively. Pupils should be able to show that they can show control in linking actions together.

The body's posture and use are more evident during whole body movements such as bending, stretching, twisting, turning and arching, than when we do the everyday actions of travelling using our legs.

These whole body movements are also performed slowly which means that they can be performed thoughtfully and to the limits of the joints concerned.

In the 'Kittens' dance, the movements are used to express the typical movement characteristics of a young animal recently born in spring. Pupils are asked to be conscious of their posture and to be aware of the repeating patterns of joined up movements as an aid to remembering, repeating and improving the dance with all its contrasts of action and use of space.

Lesson Plan – 30 minutes

Theme:
Traditional dance.

WARM-UP ACTIVITIES - 5 minutes

1 Join hands with your partner in a big circle. Stand, side by side, all facing anti-clockwise.

2 Travel round in the circle with eight skipping steps.

3 Face your partner, without touching, and do four setting steps. (Step to right, close left to right, step on right; Step to left, close right to left, step on left.) 1 . . . . 2, 3; 2 . . . . 2, 3; right . . . . 2, 3; left . . . . 2, 3.

4 Change places with your partner, holding hands for four counts.

5 Face your partner again and do four setting steps on the spot.

6 Change places with your partner, holding hands for four counts,

7 Perform eight skipping steps forwards, dancing side by side, hands joined.

Keep repeating this 32-count (4 x 8) pattern.

TEACH A DANCE - Pat-A-Cake Polka (English Folk Dance) - 20 minutes

Music *Pat-A-Cake Polka* by Blue Mountain Band (EFDS), from *Community Dances Manual 1*.

Formation A double circle with boys' backs to the centre. Directions given are those of the dancer on the inside of the circle.

Figure A Boys, hold both of your partners' hands, facing sideways. Moving anti-clockwise, dance 'heel and toe' and two chasse steps to the boys' left. (Touch floor with leading heel, toes, then the quick chasse action, left, right, left), and repeat back again to boys' right (leading heel and toe each time).

Repeat the whole movement, using a good spring at the start of each movement. 'Heel, toe, chasse, 2, 3; heel, toe, 1, 2, 3.'

Figure B Partners clap right hands together three times.
Partners clap left hands together three times.
Partners clap both hands together three times.
Partners clap own knees three times.

Figure C Boy turns partner round for four counts to the starting position to repeat the dance, or does a quick two-count turn followed by boy moving on one place, anti-clockwise, to make the dance progressive, dancing next with a new partner.

Repeat.

REVISE A FAVOURITE DANCE - 5 minutes

To provide the variety and contrast which is always an attractive feature of a dance lesson, it is recommended that this dance is not danced in a circle formation. Ideally, also, it will be one of a more modern, creative, less traditional type.

LESSON NOTES AND NC GUIDANCE

Pupils should be taught to perform movements or patterns, including some from existing dance traditions and different times and cultures. Pupils should be able to show that they can show control in linking actions together in ways that suit the activities.

The dance has an A : B : C, repeating pattern of movement actions that are linked together. 'A' is the chasse left and right, twice. 'B' is the quick handclapping. 'C' is the turning with your partner, back to your own place, ready to start again. The NC required patterns of movement and the linking of actions together are both well represented in this, as in all traditional dances.

Because of the high speed of this dance, it is essential that the teacher vocally accompanies the actions, phrase by phrase, as a reminder of the actions and, more importantly, of their high speed. 'Heel, toe, side, 2, 3; heel, toe, side, 2, 3; heel, toe, chasse left; heel, toe, chasse right', and (clapping) 'Right, 2, 3; left, 2, 3; both, 2, 3; knees', both of which will be helped further by the teacher joining in with the actions.

Lesson Plan – 30 minutes

Theme:
Friendships.

WARM-UP ACTIVITIES - 5 minutes

1 Let's remind ourselves of the friendly way we all joined hands and sang and moved together when you first came to school.

Let's join hands in one big ring,
Let's join hands and let us sing,
Let's join hands, both high and low, (reaching up, then down)
Let's drop hands and wave 'Hello!'

2 Well done. Now another friendly activity – skip to this lively, jazzy music for eight counts, then change direction and go off again for eight counts. Skip, 2, 3, 4, 5, 6, change direction; skip, 2, 3, 4, 5, 6, change again; skip, 2, 3, 4, 5, 6, 7, stop!

3 Now we are going to add meeting and giving a friendly touch to someone coming towards you, saying 'Hello! Hello!' Ready? Keep thinking! Skip, 2, 3, 4, 5, 6, change direction; skip, 2, 3, 4, 5, meet and 'Hello! Hello!'; skip, 2, 3, 4, 5, 6, change direction; skip, 2, 3, 4, 5, meet and 'Hello! Hello' – keep going!

MOVEMENT SKILLS TRAINING - 10 minutes

1 Think about the time you started school, maybe not knowing anyone in your class. Show me how you might have walked, skipped, run or galloped round the playground all by yourself. Everything looked very new, big and strange and you played by yourself. You weren't sure who you would like as your new friends. Off you go.

2 Walk in and out of one another, looking at those coming towards you. Show me a friendly gesture that you can make as you pass near to someone. You can smile, nod your head, wave.

3 When I beat the drum, stop and make a friendly contact with the nearest person. It can be flat hand to hand; a handshake; a friendly touch on the shoulder; elbow to elbow; two hands to two hands.

4 As you grew older you became good at playing with others. Find a partner you like to be with. Sit down and decide what shared activity you enjoy doing. Throwing and catching; skipping with one rope; follow my leader; skipping, side by side, with or without a rope; walking, arm in arm; or dancing about together. Decide. Stand. Practise. Go!

DANCE - Friendships - 15 minutes

1 Well done. What a lot of friendly, good fun ideas I saw and enjoyed! Have another short discussion together to see if you can agree a repeating, three- or four-part pattern to make your sequence even more interesting to perform or watch. For example – skip on the spot; travel forwards, skipping; turn round, skipping; turn round, skipping; forwards, skip together, go! Each of you can suggest one or two ideas for your shared, repeating, friendly partner activity. Please start practising as soon as you are ready.

2 Well done. As I watched you practising, I could see your little repeating patterns improving each time. Remember your pattern for later. Now go to stand by yourself, maybe a little bit shy, for the start of our 'Friendships' dance, pretending it is your first day in this school. I will remind you of the parts of the dance which we have practised already.

3 Playing all by yourselves, ready, begin! Find good spaces, well away from others. Be lively, please!

4 Now change to walking in and out of one another, looking at and smiling at others passing near you. You can wave or nod your head or smile.

5 On my drum beat, stop and make a friendly contact with the nearest person. Make it gentle as well as friendly! Then move on, listening for the next drum beat (five or six contacts).

6 When my drum sounds twice, go to meet your partner and start your little repeating pattern of shared, enjoyable activity. Keep repeating and improving it.

7 Very well done, friendly couples. Let's look at and enjoy seeing each half of the class in turn, demonstrating the last part of the dance. Watch, then tell me what you enjoyed about any of the repeating patterns.

8 Thank you for your excellent performances and your friendly, helpful comments.

9 You have done lots of moving together in this hall. I think that all these lessons, moving and working together, have helped to make you the brilliant, friendly class that you are. Let's all join hands in a big, friendly class circle.

Let's join hands, getting all together, (arms swinging)
Let's join hands in a circle round,
In we skip, good friends together, (four skips into centre)
Clap our hands and turn around. (clapping, turn on the spot)

Hands joined again, keeping close together, (facing out)
Skipping back out, of we go, (back to big circle places)
Our joined up hands swing high and low, (in the big circle)
Now we shake hands (with own partner) *and say 'Hello!'*

LESSON NOTES AND NC GUIDANCE

Pupils should be able to show that they are able to involve themselves in the continuous process of planning, performing and evaluating.

Ideally, they will be working harder for longer in almost non-stop action, displaying greater control and versatility. There should be an impression of confidence, enthusiasm and enjoyment as they stamp the work with their own personality.

Useful Addresses

The English Folk Dance and Song Society
Dance books and music: Cecil Sharp House, 2 Regents Park Road, London
NW1 7AY (tel. 0207 485 2206).

The Society For International Folk Dancing
Membership Secretary: Alan Morton, 26 Durham Road, Harrow HA1 4PG. Tel 0208 427 8042.
www.sifd.org
Dance books and music: Eleanor Gordon, 92 Norbiton Avenue, Kingston upon
Thames, Surrey KT1 3QP,
Other enquiries: Jeanette Hull, Secretary, 24 The Homeland, London Road
Morden, Surrey SM4 5AS.
A list of general and specialist classes is obtainable from the membership
secretary. Society members are available to visit schools, clubs and classes to
teach a selection of dances.

The Royal Scottish Country Dance Society
Contact: The Secretary, 12 Coates Crescent, Edinburgh, EH3 7AF, for information on publications and
videos.
Tel: 0131 225 3854
web address: www.scottishdance.org

Index